Also by Lonnie-Sharon Williams

"The Healings - Three Stories of Miraculous Healing from Scripture"

COMING HOME

LONNIE-SHARON WILLIAMS

WESTBOW°
PRESS
A DIVISION OF THOMAS NELSON
& ZONDERVAN

WestBow Press books may be ordered through booksellers or by contacting:

WestBow Press
A Division of Thomas Nelson & Zondervan
1663 Liberty Drive
Bloomington, IN 47403
www.westbowpress.com
1 (866) 928-1240

ISBN: 978-1-4908-3075-9 (sc)
ISBN: 978-1-4908-3076-6 (e)

Library of Congress Control Number: 2014905174

Printed in the United States of America.

WestBow Press rev. date: 4/29/2014

ACKNOWLEDGEMENTS

My second book – who would have thought this would happen? The Lord has blessed me to be able to write Biblical fiction and I praise Him because others are reading them.

The old saying, "it takes a village to raise a child," is the same as "it takes a great many people to encourage and support an author." I could not have done this alone. There are so many people (too numerous to mention) who have helped me along this journey and I give my heartfelt thanks to them.

Special thanks to those who have poured positively into my life: First of all, to my Lord and Savior, Jesus Christ, who the true author of all things; to my mentor and friend, Joyce J. McIntyre, Pastor at Northeast Church of God in Cleveland; to my church family at The Church of God of Cleveland; to Bishop Leanza Ford and Lady Lisa Ford of True Faith Apostolic Bibleway Church in Cleveland; to Dr. James D. and Lady Donna Walls of Xenia 2nd Street Church of God; and to Pastor James and Lady Maryann Roma at Wintergreen Ledges Church of God in Akron. Their spiritual support, prayers, and encouragement kept me on task.

I sincerely appreciate Andrew Chess and David Horowitz for their insight into Jewish traditions; to

Michael Norwalk, a most excellent IT professional; to young readers Abigail and Samantha, along with their dad Mark Behrend for helping me during my crunch times. I also thank my best buds, Hattie Smith and Bernice Shaw, for their encouragement and helpful suggestions.

A posthumous appreciation to my late parents, Daisy and Robert Spivey, and my late aunt Orlean Spivey. I salute my five siblings for their faith in my abilities. Lastly, a big hug to my son, Robert, and his wonderful wife, Clare Graves.

Thank you so much for your pats on my back and just as you prayed for me, I am also praying for the Lord's continued blessings on you all!

> *I love to tell the story of unseen things above,*
> *Of Jesus and His glory, of Jesus and His love.*
> *I love to tell the story, because I know 'tis true;*
> *It satisfies my longings as nothing else can do.*

> *Hymn: I Love to Tell the Story*
> *Words by Katherine Hankey, Music by William G. Fischer*

COMING HOME

JAKOBI

THE STORY OF THE PRODIGAL SON
LUKE 15:11-32

JAKOBI

Characters

Jakobi (Ja-ko-bee) – Younger son of Matthan (the Prodigal)
Zyama (Zy-ah-ma) – Jakobi's mother
Matthan (Mat-than) – Jakobi's father
Eliakim (Eli-ah-kim) – Jakobi's elder brother
Hannah (Han-nah) – Eliakim's wife
Rachel (Ra-chell) – Baby sister of Jakobi
Salome (Sa-low-may)– Sister of Jakobi
Jesse and Obed - Eliakim's sons
Ruth – Baby daughter of Eliakim and Hannah
Abijah (A-bee-jah) – Jakobi's best friend
Joash (Jo-Ash) – Abijah's elder brother
Amos (A-mos) – Abijah's father
Nihomi (Ny-home-ee) –Abijah's mother
Ramani (Rah-mahn-ee) – Abijah's sister
Gupta (Gup-tah) – Head house servant
Emad-Shevets (E-mahd-shev-its) – Jakobi's Canaanite
employer
Hoshi (Ho-shee) -- Emad-Shevets' young daughter
Ezzidin (Ez-zih-den) – Cheating investor/money lender
Etufi (Ee-too-fee) – One of Emad-Shevets' pig servants
Ranal – Heber – Guron – Other pig servants of Emad-Shevets
Banna and sons, Ezra and Abni and Simon - Jakobi's servants

PROLOGUE

Eliakim struggled to pull his 11-year old brother from the muddy ditch. He tried to tell Jakobi the area was much too muddy for him to run very fast. His sandals were made for indoors, not for the hilly ground and mud that was filled with puddles from the recent rain. As for himself, he wore comfortable laced sandals that wound around his calf.

"Ah," he thought, "you can't tell this boy anything, because he will not listen. I told him to either wear laced sandals that would allow him to go up into the hills or to be barefoot. Will he ever learn? Even the shepherds do not wear their wrap sandals after a heavy rain."

Eliakim gave a great sigh as he continued to try to free the boy from the mud.

"Jakobi, dig your toes into the mud and push your body upward so I can lift you out! You're way too heavy to lift!"

His younger brother finally did as he was told and Eliakim pulled him out of the thick mud. Jakobi smiled to himself as the mud released him, making a loud sucking noise. He stomped his feet a few times to try to eliminate the thick globs that were plastered around his toes. Laughing, he continued beside his elder brother as they walked the lane to the inner fields and headed toward home.

The shepherds stopped what they were doing and smiled as they watched the two brothers leave the hillside and head toward home. The saw the elder boy reach over and touched the younger brother's head to rumple his hair lovingly as they walked.

Eliakim pointed to the hillside and smiled. "Look, the new lambs are next to their mothers. Aren't they a beautiful sight? That spotted one next to the tree is a frisky ram and will help to give me a healthy herd. See the fluffy ewe where the shepherd is standing? That's another one I've already picked out. I've already told father that I'm ready."

Jakobi nodded, but did not say anything. You'd think Eliakim had nothing else to do but gaze at different sized sheep. Just because he was six years older than himself did not mean he was stupid about raising sheep.

"I know what you're thinking, little brother, but one day I'll have many sheep on my hills also. Did I tell you I finally saved up enough of my allowance and have purchased property on the border of father's land? Father said when I am able to purchase the land, he would give me a small amount of sheep to start my own herd. He has even allowed me to pick the ones I want." His brother's happiness was overflowing.

Jakobi smiled and jokingly asked, "Have you named each of the sheep you've already picked?"

Eliakim chuckled in return and quickly replied, "Well, some I have. Laugh if you wish, but soon I'll have enough land and herds to marry Hannah."

"You haven't even talked to father about this yet," replied Jakobi. "Has he spoken with Hannah's family yet?"

"No, but both of our parents know we're in favor of the alliance. I know Mother will be more than pleased for she and Hannah's mother are great friends. And Hannah is beautiful and smart and knows as many things as her brothers. I believe she must have been listening when her brothers were being taught business matters. She is certainly a prize!"

Eliakim rambled on and on about Hannah's beauty and virtues until Jakobi's mind began to block out his brother's conversation. He sighed and continued trudging along, following his brother.

"Are we going to be on this hillside for long? I hope not because I'm hungry and my backside is wet and my feet are beginning to feel squishy." Jakobi swiped at the plastered mud on his robe and bent to remove more of it from his sandals.

"No, I guess we'd better return home now. I can see you're very uncomfortable in your clothing. You'd better see if Gupta will be able to have one of the servants try to repair those sandals."

Slowly, the two started back down the hillside, trying to remain upright on the grassy knoll. Reaching the bottom, they entered the house from the rear so as not to be seen by their mother, Zyama. The robe Jakobi wore was one of the newer ones his mother recently purchased from the traders and he did not want to run into her until he and his brother were free of mud.

Their father's head servant, Gupta, looked over at the two and shook his head. He called for one of the male servants who came and stood ready with a change of clothing for both Eliakim and Jakobi as the two entered the back room where their feet could be washed by another servant. A bath would be prepared for them both in the back dressing room.

"As soon as I'm able, I'll hire a few servants, too." Eliakim mused, more to himself, than to his brother. "A household needs at least a few servants. I won't need as many as our parents have, but I will need a few."

Again, Jakobi smiled but did not say anything, knowing his brother did not expect a response.

Let Eliakim have his dreams, he thought.

1

Jakobi meditated with his throbbing head in his hands as he sat on a rock in the western field, one of the many fields that were owned by his father, Matthan. He had just returned from a rousing celebration given by his friend that lasted through the night and into this morning. He had not been home as yet and the sun was just coming over the horizon.

It had been his intent to return sober this morning for he had promised his father. And, sadly, just as his father had predicted, Jakobi had drunk his fill of fine wine and eaten the gourmet food presented by his friend, Abijah.

Abijah was also a second son, but he seemed to always have money and his father seemed to be more lenient than his own.

"Drink up," he would laughingly say, "there's more where that came from."

His friend wore rich colors and came and went as he pleased. Why, he even had a few servants and two slaves, which he purchased with his own money. A few weeks before he had given both slaves their freedom. However, out of gratitude they chose to stay with him. His father must have given him free reign over a great amount of funds. Jakobi knew like himself, Abijah was still at an age where he received an allowance each month and he presumed it had to be at least ten times larger than his own.

All he could think about was the fact that many of his friends seemed to be able to do more than he ever could. He was the second son of his father and he knew he would only inherit a portion of his father's wealth.

His brother, Eliakim, was the eldest and heir, and would inherit a double portion. He was not envious of his brother, for it was the way of Jews that the eldest would receive the double portion.

He had sisters, but he knew they would probably marry very well since the eldest of the two, Salome, was sure to soon have her eyes on another well-to-do young man. Little Rachel was the youngest and she could always wrap her finger around her father and get whatever she wanted.

His mother was a dutiful wife and was able to shop whenever and wherever she pleased, yet she was very frugal. She never shopped for the sake of shopping, but only when something was needed for the house or if an item needed to be replaced. His father was very open with giving her money to shop for he knew his wife would never overspend on any item.

He put his thoughts to his elder brother, Eliakim, and his wife, Hannah. Hannah was not only beautiful but also had a good business head on her shoulders and was instrumental in some of his brother's decisions. They had two children and their two sons were helpful to their father. Eliakim's eldest son would soon celebrate his bar mitzvah and was helpful in running his father's property, and the younger one enjoyed working with figures and would stand beside his father learning the sale of crops and animals.

Eliakim had a few years of wildness as a young man, but settled down quickly when he fell in love with Hannah. Jakobi was young when his brother married, but he remembered well the betrothal process of his elder brother. His mother and father had made a wise decision when considering the type of woman Eliakim would want. Of course Eliakim had already met with many of the lovely eligible girls in the area (compliments of his mother who wanted only the best for her eldest son), but it was clear that Eliakim preferred Hannah over all the others. It was also clear from her response that Hannah also preferred Eliakim, for they had known each other since childhood and their mothers were good friends.

When Matthan went to confer with Hannah's father for a match, her father was very happy to see him. It did not take long for them both to realize the union of their families would be advantageous to both. At Eliakim and Hannah's betrothal, all could see it was indeed a love match and they were married within the next year.

2

Jakobi's thoughts turned to Ramani, Abijah's lovely sister, who was a few years under him. She was also a few years younger than himself, but already she was a beauty. He remembered seeing her as a skinny girl with big, long-lashed brown eyes and long beautiful hair that was a deep honey color. She was growing into a beautiful young woman with a smooth flawless complexion, long silky hair, huge brown eyes and a slim figure. He knew she would make a wonderful wife for someone. She was intelligent, witty, had a smile that lit up the room, and had a throaty laugh that made you want to laugh with her. She had started wearing the veil that partially hid her face, but not her wonderful eyes.

Abijah was very protective of his sister. Jakobi knew Abijah had the same thoughts he had for his own sisters. His friend felt no one was good enough for Ramani just as he also felt no one was good enough for Salome or Rachel.

Ramani's father did not have to worry about the wrong type of man asking for her for Abijah scrutinized every male that came into the household. He loved his sibling and would not allow anything or anyone to make her sad, worried, or harmed in any way.

Jakobi laughed to himself. He knew that even he did not measure up to the standards Abijah set for the future husband of Ramani. If it were possible, Abijah would not allow her to marry and would move her into his own house before the wrong type of suitor asked for her hand.

Jakobi remembered mentioning to Abijah how pretty Ramani was looking on a particular day and Abijah gave him a quelling look, letting him know to stop looking at his sister.

And Ramani equally loved her brother. Whatever he said, she listened and agreed with him. The lucky man would have the blessings of the good Lord and Abijah if he was able to court and marry her.

Shaking himself, he knew he had lagged too long. When he thought he was sober enough, Jakobi decided it was now time to head for home.

The shepherds in the fields stopped what they were doing and watched as he wobbled a bit and began the trek to his father's house. The house servants and older shepherds pointed out Jakobi to the younger servants and used him as an example to them of what happens when your lifestyle is not as it should be. Jakobi was pitiful in their eyes and a disgrace to his parents.

The shepherds were loyal to Matthan and knew it was unwise to disgrace the master in such a way. All felt Matthan was a good man and deserved better. They believed it was good that he had another son who was obedient in every way. In their eyes it was good that Jakobi was not the eldest.

Yet, there were many younger servants who still liked Jakobi, for he was less serious and enjoyed life, although they did not entirely agree with his lifestyle. Being a handsome and frivolous young man, he attracted the wrong type of women and men friends.

When he finally walked into the house, Jakobi met his mother coming from the kitchen with two of her maids.

"Oh, Jakobi," Zyama cried, "do not upset your father today. He waited up most of the night because he wanted to talk with you. And now, look at you. Go to your room and clean up."

As she hugged her son, Zyama then told one of her servants to have water brought to his room to wash and to have the kitchen fix a light meal for him and lay out a clean robe.

3

As he headed toward his bedroom, Jakobi made a decision. He needed to leave this house. His brother was the beloved son and he was being smothered by his mother; his sisters ignored him and had their own friends. His father did not seem to notice his discontent and it was time to strike out on his own. Many young men left home to make their fortune, he thought.

After washing, changing his clothing and sitting down to eat, he rehearsed in his mind what he planned to present to his father.

Just as he finished wiping his mouth, Matthan came and sat across from him in the eating area on a small stool.

"Father," he started, "I would like to speak with you."

"And I, you," his father replied. "The way you live is not befitting a son of mine. You need to try to settle down and think about marriage. You are not betrothed to any of the women in town even though you could be. There are many young women who have had their eyes on you. I could easily make a betrothal contract with any of their fathers today if you would like."

"I'm not interested in any of them. As the second son, I have little to offer them."

His father sat back in his chair and rubbed his beard as he responded. "You will still have a great inheritance for I am not a poor man, and although your brother will inherit as the eldest, you will still see a great deal of wealth. Your allowance is not small and it was your mother who suggested the last raise you received."

"You should remember that I was the third son of my father. I did not get rich by carousing with my friends. I used my allowance to purchase healthy sheep and cattle. With the money from raising my livestock and their sale, I was able to purchase the land we live on and added more property over the years. I am able to pay my servants a livable wage and they live comfortably. I was not always rich, son. If you start now, you could become wealthy yourself, but first you need to think about your future."

"I have, father," he quietly replied. "I would like to have my inheritance now to do as I wish. I have watched my friends do as they please and I want more freedom."

Matthan looked incredulously at his son. He could not believe his ears.

"I am not dead yet, Jakobi," he flatly stated. "Why would you want your inheritance now? Your allowance is sufficient to make some investments for yourself and to begin living as a wise young man. If only you would try to do something with yourself."

Jakobi put his head down and repeated, "I would like my share of the inheritance now to do as I wish. When I leave, you will not be left alone. You already have Eliakim and he will inherit greatly when you die, whereas I will get my so-called 'second son's' inheritance. I am quite sure my sisters will receive a more than satisfactory dowry and will marry well."

"You will get a great deal, for as I said, I am not a poor man."

His father was incensed! Matthan stood up and gritting his teeth, said, "Think about what you have asked. If you think money will be the answer to your unrest, you are wrong. You acquaint yourself with friends who seem to have it all, but money can't buy friendship or loyalty. However, if that is your request, I will have my man of business meet with me and divide land and animals."

"No father," his son replied, "I would like my inheritance in funds that I may spend when and how I wish. Land and animals cannot travel with me, for I plan to see the world outside of this area."

His father was now very angry. Jakobi was always headstrong but this was beyond the norm! Matthan abruptly left the room and went to seek his wife. After conferring with Zyama, they agreed that it would be best to let Jakobi find his own way. Both acknowledged he was a grown man and very disgruntled and would remain so if he stayed.

When Eliakim was informed of their decision, he did not say anything. There was nothing he could say to settle the issue. Bsides, even if he tried to convince his brother that what he was asking was not good, he knew his viewpoint would not be heard. He felt Jakobi had always been envious that he was the second son and not the first.

Jakobi was always headstrong and had become quite lazy, allowing the servants to perform some of his chores when he had a party to attend, or just did not want to do the work.

Eliakim left the house and headed for the cattle stalls.

4

Gupta found Eliakim in the stalls but left him alone to his own misery. The house servants had previously informed Gupta of what they had overheard during the conversation between Matthan and Jakobi. Rather than make any judgments or take sides, they kept their thoughts to themselves, but reported what they heard to Gupta, the head servant who reported directly to Matthan and Eliakim.

However, no matter what took place between the two brothers, Gupta was more loyal to Eliakim. He had watched Eliakim and Jakobi grow to manhood and he did not approve of the younger man's actions. As Matthan's first-born son, Eliakim was always circumspect in his dealings with the traders, the community, the servants, the shepherds, and even the slaves. For years he had watched Eliakim put up with Jakobi's misdeeds, even when he was sometimes blamed for his younger brother's mistakes.

Eliakim only nodded to Gupta; later he asked him to have his horse saddled and explained that he was going to travel to the outskirts of his father's property to check on his herds of sheep and cattle. There were things he needed to think over and he could not do it in the confines of his home, where the tension heightened as the day progressed.

5

After a few days, Matthan called both of his sons to the room where he performed business matters and had them sit.

He explained to them what he had decided and said that he had spoken with his man of business and explained that Jakobi would receive his inheritance as of this day. In the event he decided to return, he would not receive any further inheritance; for all income as of today and afterwards would go into the inheritance of Eliakim. Both said they understood.

Jakobi impatiently rocked back and forth on his heels and then asked when he would receive his inheritance for he wished to leave soon.

"It will be completely settled by tomorrow morning." Matthan looked from one son to the other.

"I didn't think this matter would have taken so long. I really wanted to get this settled so I could leave," he muttered.

Neither his father nor his elder brother looked surprised but Matthan's heart fell. How soon? he wondered.

"That is good. I will be leaving in two to three days time," Jakobi announced, which shocked both father and elder son. However, neither said anything to him.

"All right; you will receive it tomorrow evening in silver and gold," said Matthan. "The servants will begin putting your money into packets following the midday meal to make it easy to carry on your mules. I presume you've already picked the ones you are going to use and have informed Gupta. I am quite sure he will get together with the grooms."

Eliakim nodded his head and left the room behind Jakobi.

After picking up what he thought was a small rock, Matthan realized it was one of the family rings worn by each of his sons. Unknowingly Jakobi had calmly placed his ring on the table. With a hurting heart, he placed it in the money pouch tied around his waist and slowly followed behind his elder son.

Days later, the only ones to say their goodbyes to him were Jakobi's sisters and his mother. The worse part of it was Zyama cried into his shoulder and his sisters looked crestfallen after kissing his cheeks. Father had told them this was his decision.

In early afternoon, Jakobi left without sitting with his family for the mid-day meal. Two mules and his horse were loaded with his money, clothing, and other personal effects as he headed toward the edge of town. His mother and sisters again hugged him and sobbed as they whispered in this ears before he mounted his horse.

His father's servants watched as Jakobi left the homestead leading the mules behind him. There was talk among the house servants of Jakobi's decision to leave, taking his inheritance with him.

Silently house servants, field servants, and shepherds observed his departure and soon went back to their duties.

* * *

Jakobi let his horse lead the way as his mules trodded on behind him. He passed calm ponds and turbulent rivers and paid to use ferries to take him across. He was not worried about the weather and when it rained he stayed at inns along the way.

He wasn't sure where he was going and thought he'd know where to settle when he reached a city of his choice. The weather was balmy and he stopped each day to let his animals rest. Never having been away from home for long periods of time, he took full advantage of looking at the various towns and sceneries.

Once, he followed a caravan for a full day, turning off the roads to travel to his unknown destination. The tribal leader warned him of highway thieves along the way and advised him to always stick to the most traveled roads.

"Beware of mountains, my son, for they hide wild animals and bandits," he admonished. "Many bad men waylay travelers who are unaware they are hiding in the hills. They have been known to rob and beat travelers and leave them bleeding along the roads. Then there are the lepers. You should take care. You look like a young man from a well-to-do family. It would be wise for you to exercise caution.

For a few days, Jakobi realized that traveling alone with a beautiful horse and healthy mules with money in their sacks was not the best idea he had ever had, but Yahweh blessed him with a safe journey.

6

Over 15 months' time, Jakobi had traveled through Galilee into Amman and then on to Samaria. He had left his money with a holding house manager by the name of Ezziddin in a small town in Samaria and began spending his inheritance bit by bit. With Ezziddin's help, he rented a small house on the outskirts. Whenever he was low on funds, he traveled to Ezziddin's business to withdraw some of his funds.

Ezziddin was considered an "investment banker" in the town and doled out the money he held whenever Jakobi asked. However, he never fully read the contract the man had written out for him and it was not until later that he understood Ezziddin also took his "cut". In his presence, the banker immediately advised him that he would always be charged a fee for his handling of the money. Jakobi did not really pay attention to what he was saying and felt he had enough inheritance to take care of his needs.

Jakobi met and made a few friends like himself. He partied, drank, and used the Samaritan harlots to his pleasure. "This is the life!"

He had never known such freedom before and it was a heady feeling. There was no one to chastise him; he came and went as he pleased, and he had friends that he picked himself.

"This must be how Abijah feels," he thought. Abijah was a second son, but he seemed to always have money. It was not doled out to him by his father as Matthan did to him. He made sure his friends ate and drank at the parties he held in his rented house.

Although there was a Jewish synagogue within a mile of where he was staying, he seldom attended, perhaps once every few months or so. It wasn't long before he quit attending completely. If Yahweh was supposed to be a merciful God, then that meant he would always be protected by the Lord whether he went to synagogue or not. He was a Jew and, of course, Jews were the the Lord's 'chosen' people.

He did feel a little guilty when he stopped attending because his mother had ingrained it into him that he should attend services. Yes, he was a part of the Chosen People, but there were certain things Yahweh expected of him, she would say.

Jakobi began to realize his money was depleting, so he scaled back on some of his spending. Soon he knew it was time to begin selling one of his mules. One by one he sold the three mules he brought with him. He loved his horse and waited until he could no longer support the animal. At the last, he sold his horse to an Ethiopian trader for a song.

Next he began selling some of his fashionable clothing until eventually, he did not look like the son of a rich man. His hair and once-trimmed beard had begun to lengthen and he decided to let them grow.

As the second year wore on, some of his new friends slowly began to desert him when it became apparent he had little or no money to spend on them. At one point he tried borrowing from them, but they would not even loan him a few coins to purchase his bare necessities.

It soon became apparent to him that Ezziddin's cut was not a small percentage, but a very large amount. The moneyholder had gone through Jakobi's money much faster than Jakobi himself.

Finally, when Jakobi went to get what was left of his monthly allotment from Ezziddin, he was shocked to learn he was virtually broke.

"Things like this just happen. It happens to all of us," Ezziddin quietly explained. He shot Jakobi a sorrowful look and explained that there was nothing he could do. And no, he could not lend him credit for, after all, Jakobi was broke. How would he be able to pay back the funds?

"How could so much money go so fast?" Jakobi was in a quandry. It did not take long for him to realize that Samaria was not known for being fair to outsiders, and working with a conniving money handler was not a good idea. He should have checked Ezziddin out before investing his money with him. He wondered if his father had ever transacted business with such a charlatan. Of course not. Father had a good business head, as did his brother Eliakim. Plus, he read his contracts from start to finish, so he would understand the legal ramifications.

There were times he even talked with his wife about various issues.

Many times Eliakim had told him he should sit with his father and learn how to purchase property and animals; how to hire loyal servants, and other business transactions. Eliakim had been taught these things and he was a man after his father's heart. But, being the man he was, Jakobi refused to listen to his elder brother or his father.

Too late, he thought, too late!

7

Once again Spring arrived as well as a famine. It had not rained for some time, and the newly planted crops were not coming up. What few plants that struggled to come out of the ground had begun to shrivel from the heat. With very little money on him, Jakobi realized he would starve to death if something was not done soon.

He traveled into Canaanite territory but could not find employment. He had no skills to offer, but luckily knew how to raise cattle and sheep. No one had need of a shepherd or herder and after searching through many areas, he was hired to work in the fields of a man who raised cattle and pigs. His employer did not need someone for his cattle, but had a position for working with pigs.

Working with pigs was his only alternative and he was desperate. Jews did not raise pigs. Jakobi did not like pigs. He neither touched pigs nor ate their meat, but he knew he had to take the position since it was the only one he'd found available. Emad-Shevets spoke Aramaic and a few other languages, but mostly Aramaic to be understood by his servants.

Emad-Shevets was not a man he would normally want to have as his employer, but no one else would hire him

— for he was a Jew. His job was to feed the pigs and clean behind their waste. Not a pretty job, but at least it gave him a few denarii and he was able to sleep in the stable-like building. The workers had mats that were laid out in two lines on the floor and the building was dry and not badly constructed.

Jakobi never before knew how horrible the smell of pigs could be. Being Jewish, his father did not raise pigs and, besides, Matthan had servants to clean behind the cattle and horses.

Slop. Pig slop. That was what the other servants called the food the pigs ate. Leftovers from Emad-Shevets' table, grain, mash and the dirty water the pigs wallowed in – all mixed together. And those stupid pigs gloried in their meals – snorting and groveling with glee! Yecch!

It didn't take long for him to realize Emad-Shevets did not feed his servants decent food. At times Jakobi went without meals because he could hardly stomach what was presented before him.

Once, being faint with hunger, Jakobi fell into a small pond. He could swim, thank the good Lord for his older brother's tutelage. He swam to the area where he could feel the muddy bottom under his feet. When the water around him became still, he chanced to look at his reflection and realized he had lost some weight and his face was beginning to look haggard.

He knew if his "use-to-be" Samaritan friends could see him now, he was sure they would turn their backs or walk another way. As long as he had coins, he had friends.

The only 'friend' he recognized was another pig worker by the name of Etufi, as well as the other pig co-workers he considered companions. He was not sure of Etufi's nationality but they were able to easily communicate and seemed to have lived similar lifestyles.

He could not think of Emad-Shevets' ugly daughter, Hoshi, as a friend. She constantly came around the pig sty to make sure he was working or trying to make conversation. Since he did not report to her but to her father, he generally ignored her. There was no way he would have anything to do with her.

Twice, when he saw her coming toward the styes, he turned and went toward the stables in order to avoid her for he knew Hoshi's father did not allow her near the stables and especially near the pig workers.

Not only did he think she was ugly in his eyes, but she smelled just like the pigs, emanating an odd odor that no decent Jewish girl would ever have on her body. Even harlots smelled better. Didn't she know about bathing or using body oils or spices? But then, too, her mother carried the same aroma. Perhaps that odor was their perfume, he was not sure.

There was no way he wanted to have anything to do with her and it was not just the fact that she was a Canaanite. Her hair was straggly and even her fingernails stayed dirty, which made him wonder if she ever bathed at all. But who was he to think that? He hardly bathed himself nowadays.

Yet, Emad-Shevets believed his daughter to be the loveliest girl in the area. That certainly was his opinion, Jakobi thought to himself.

Her father had to be blind!

A few of the male servants had shown an interest in Hoshi, but Emad-Shevets had fired two of them for getting too close to her.

Once, a male house servant grabbed her arm to keep her from falling into a ditch made by the runoffs from a rainstorm, and he had a lot of explaining to do. Feeling thankful for being kept from harm, Hoshi explained to her father about the ditch that was close to the house and how the servant had saved her from a bad fall. The very next day three servants were sent to fill in the ditch with rocks and dirt and the one who had saved her was later transferred to work in the fields.

Emad-Shevets thanked the man, but before the week was out, he began working in the field in an area farthest from the house.

Hoshi had very few female friends, but had many suitors from the nearby villages. Since her father was quite well off, she would probably marry well. He knew a few of the younger, as well as older men wanted to set up betrothal agreements, but Emad-Shevets was taking his time, checking out these prospective suitors.

Because of his wealth, his daughter's hand brought numerous suitors and invitations to parties and vast amounts of presents for him and his wife. Hoshi received beautifully made sandals, exquisite scarves and shawls, bracelets of expensive stones and sparkling rings.

Jakobi was not so dumb to not realize that Emad-Shevets was looking to the highest bidder for his daughter.

He entertained the 'chosen' with excellent food, wine and hospitality as he quietly interviewed each suitor and his family. No love was involved in the alignment of families – just money.

Ah, he thought, my father was right – money does not buy friends! It's just that people come around you because you have money to spend on them. Is that why Abijah has so many friends? Was it because he knew he could have many friends as long as the good times lasted or he could treat them to vast amounts of good food, excellent wine and parties which would draw people around him?

As Jakobi looked back, he realized he was one of those friends because he knew he would always have a good time in Abijah's house. It also meant he would be able to gaze for a short while at Abijah's lovely sister, Ramani.

If Abijah saw him now, would he allow him to attend those gatherings if he knew of his present poverty? After thinking that over, he realized that most of the young men who attended those parties were either second, third or fourth sons, and all came from well-to do families such as himself.

Sure, Emad-Shevets could entertain, but he was a lousy employer. Jakobi's first pay amount was less than what he was told it would be. The next time, the pay amount was even lower. When he complained, Emad-Shevets smilingly told him if he did not like the pay, he was free to leave and work somewhere else, knowing no one in the area was hiring. Especially not a Jew.

Daily he sat on a big boulder and pondered all aspects of his life since he lived in his parents' home. His family would be ashamed to know that he was the keeper of pigs in an area among Canaanites. These were the same people who were not considered very welcome in his town.

Pigs! Sows and boars! Bah! Fat, ugly brutes with no self-respect! Grunting and groaning as they ate, slept or moved. They even snored when they slept. And their smell — it was horrible! And to make it even worse, he was becoming used to it!!!

Could he go any lower?

8

Eliakim was still very upset from the antics of his brother and could see what his absence was doing to his family. Why couldn't Jakobi just act right? He was an embarrassment to his father, mother and sisters, but especially to him. His friends still tease him about his younger brother. He remembered how the servants had observed what went on in the household of Matthan and was aware of what they thought of Jakobi.

He'd heard his father tell his brother to slow down on staying out late each night and to consider getting new friends. Jakobi's friends loved to party and they always brought women with them.

He considered what his mother had expressed. "There are so many decent girls in the area; lovely and refined; why doesn't Jakobi at least look at them?"

Yet who did Jakobi cavort with? Whores!! Even though his brother said he and Abijah never had relations with any of them, the temptation might one day become too great. Many men have contracted strange diseases from those whores! He had a few friends who developed problems in their pubic areas after sleeping with them. Jakobi needed to think about getting his life together, settling down and marrying.

He knew marriage was not always the answer to everything, but he did know that a good woman was instrumental to a man's maturity and welfare. He experienced settling down and enjoying it from his own marriage to Hannah. She was a calming force, wise and, he believed, understood business as well as he, if not more.

She was the only daughter with three brothers and her parents raised her to understand business dealings along with her brothers. Her insight had helped him many times in his business dealings. There were times he discussed his decisions with her to see what she thought of them.

Matthan had been trying very hard to get his younger son to think responsibly, even to the point of raising his allowance in order for his son to think of investing for the future. But Jakobi used the bulk of his money to provide food and wine for his friends. Even the men who advised Eliakim on his investments volunteered their services to Jakobi, but the idiot refused.

What kind of life was his brother looking for? What type of future had he hoped to gain by taking his inheritance? If he was so interested in money, why take it now? Chances are, he would outlive his father and would see a greater share than his second son allotment at the present time. His father had already explained to him that any proceeds received from the date of his leaving would all go to Eliakim, with nothing more to Jakobi. Every day his father's investments increased and would belong to him on his father's death. Not that he wanted his father to die – oh no, he loved his father – but everyone knew that man was meant to be born and then live out his years and then die.

That was man's heritage. Yahweh had order to everything and living and dying was part of life.

Gupta knew Eliakim's feelings and had not said anything to him. Eliakim loved Gupta as if he was an older brother. He had served under Matthan since a teenager and later became head servant. In fact Gupta's wife, Semenya, had been one of the midwives at their births.

He felt the problem with Jakobi stemmed from the fact that he was not brought up under the same disciplinary rules as he. Now that Jakobi was older, his parents thought he should fall in line behind his brother, but they had not exerted the same authority on their two sons.

Gupta was not a wealthy servant, but he had a wealth of integrity and Matthan relied on him and his wisdom in the running of his household. He had tried his utmost to use the same discipline on each of his three sons. Thus far, they had not given him or his wife the problems Eliakim's brother had given their father.

The servants under Gupta had great respect for him and he not only kept Matthan's family secrets, but also kept the servants' secrets. Many of the servants owed him their jobs — for when an indiscretion was made by any of them, he did not always report it to Matthan, but handled the affair himself. When it was a serious offense, he took it upon himself to get the perpetrator away from the house. He would later report it to Matthan and make arrangements for that person's replacement. When it came to the business of the household, Gupta was a shrewd manager.

Gupta passed through the main part of the household on his way to the kitchens and saw Eliakim in the main room. Eliakim hailed him and smiled at his friend. He noticed that for the last few years, Eliakim's smile did not reach his eyes.

As he did every day for the last few years, Eliakim asked if any of the servants had heard any news of his brother. The servants' grapevine in the household, shepherds, and those from other households were known to meet, converse and exchange news most days. He knew if any servants had heard any news, they would report it to Gupta.

And every day, Gupta's answer was always the same: "No, no one has heard anything."

9

He looked up when he saw movement in the distance. Emad-Shevets slowly walked his fat body toward him in the field, chewing on a piece of hay.

"Jakobi," he shouted, "I will need you to go into town and purchase some more grain for my pigs. I had previously spoken with the grain merchant and he sent a messenger to tell me he has the bags ready for me. Here is a pouch of money that will get enough grain to last a while."

Jakobi looked at the pouch and visions of himself running away with Emad-Shevets' money came into his head. As he looked at his employer, he could see that he was scrutizing him in return. Does he think I will steal the money? No, he thought, it's bad enough that I'm poor; I will not become a thief!

He quietly took the money and placed it in his girdle and smiled, saying he would harness the donkeys to pull the small wagon that would carry the grain back to the farm. Emad-Shevets gave directions to the area in town where the merchants sold grain and old wheat for the field areas. Jakobi repeated the directions and nodded his head that he would leave right away.

Once again temptation reared its head as he felt the bag of coins. He would not be the first person to steal an employer's money and no one would know if he took a few coins. Besides, Emad-Shevets was no better than Ezzidin. His employer owed him more wages than he was getting.

He dismissed the thought right away. His God would know.

Heading toward the stables, he began to pick up his pace. He would be away from the pigs and the farm for the day. Since it had been some time since he'd gone into town, he was beginning to look forward to the trip. Remembering the last time he had been in a town area, he smiled. When he was in Samaria, he still had a lot of money and could give lavish parties with the money from his father.

Then his thoughts went to Ezzidin and how the crooked investor used his funds for his own gain. Ezzidin practiced usury, which was not allowed according to Mosaic Law, but even he was aware that both Jews and Gentile alike used this corrupt form of practice. Jakobi realized he was naïve in the ways of business, but was quickly learning about such things. He had heard of dealings such as his own, but never expected to experience this form of corruption.

He remembered when he was younger how a friend of his father's had visited his home for advice from Matthan. The man was crying and complained that he was ruined. He had asked Matthan for advice prior to making a deal with a trader, whom he did not know very well. Matthan had given him good advice, but the man had later consulted one of his own acquaintances and, to his detriment, followed the acquaintance's advice. Once his money was depleted, he had returned to Matthan hoping Matthan could help him figure out how to get his money back.

Matthan sadly informed him there was nothing he could do. After all, a deal is a deal. His father never said a chiding word to the man that he should have listened to the advice of a friend, not the advice from a person who was not a friend. He should have known a friend would always give a friend good advice.

Although he was no longer a religious person (since there wasn't a Jewish synagogue nearby, and he had not been to a worship service in some time), he felt Yahweh was beginning to look out for him.

It's strange, he thought, when things go wrong how one tends to look to the religious teachings with which he was raised. When he was in the religious school, the rabbi would poke him with a long stick and admonish him to listen because one day in the future he would need the Lord.

That future time had now come.

10

Jakobi began to sing one of the first worship psalms he remembered since leaving his home. It was the very last worship service he attended with his family prior to leaving home and lately it had been running through his mind.

Since he had left the family home, he began calling on the strength of Yahweh and what he had learned in his Hebrew classes and past temple services. When he was really down in the dumps, humming or singing the hymns seemed to calm him, even though generally he was not interested in the music and only attended services with the family to appease his mother.

Lately he had been praying to Yahweh, expressing the hurt he had been feeling – to the point of making up his own words to the music — because he had forgotten some of the original words. However, there was one song he loved that was sung in the synagogue during his youth as well as at his bar mitzvah. For some reason the words had stuck in his heart and mind. Now that he was at his lowest point, the song came back to him:

"Give ear to my words, O Yahweh; give heed to
my groaning and harken to the
sound of my cries.

You are my King and my God, for to
You do I pray.
Oh Yahweh, in the morning You hear my voice;
in the morning I prepare a sacrifice for
You and watch." *

"Too much! Too much!" he groaned, putting his hands on both sides of his face.

"I don't even have a sacrifice to give you, Lord."

There was nothing he could do to help his situation. Jakobi knew he had brought his problems on himself. He should have listened to his family, but realized his stubbornness as well as his pride were two of his main problems.

11

As he clicked his tongue to urge the slowly plodding donkeys forward, he heard a wagon approaching from behind. When he turned to see, he could tell by its construction that someone of wealth was coming toward him. Once again he began clicking at the donkeys, edging his wagon to the side of the road in order to allow the other wagon to pass.

Three men were in the passing wagon and one of the passengers in the wagon looked vaguely familiar. To his surprise, Jakobi realized it was his friend, Abijah, and two older men. A servant was in front holding the reins as he drove two beautiful horses.

At first he hoped he would not be recognized, but in his heart knew it was wonderful to see someone from his hometown. As they passed, Abijah turned around and stared.

"Jakobi! Is that you?" Quickly Abijah turned, said something to the men, then jumped from the wagon and ran back toward Jakobi. He caught up with the wagon, jumped into the backboard and crawled forward. Lifting his robe, he climbed into the seat next to his friend and hugged him.

"I cannot believe it is you." Abijah grabbed his shoulders and kissed him on each cheek while he looked searchingly in his friend's face.

"You look haggard and your beard is scraggly! And my, how you've lost weight! I almost did not recognize you!"

Jakobi lowered his head, embarrassed by the scrutiny.

"My, my, I really did not recognize you; it has been so long." Abijah again hugged his friend. "My goodness, you smell of pigs!" He held his nose for effect.

Always a talker, Abijah filled Jakobi in on news of the town and its people, those of his friends who were now married or betrothed since he left home, and finally his family.

"At first I thought you had died. Your family is in mourning, Jakobi. I asked your brother about you and he would only say the family had not heard from you for awhile. I thought you had just gone on a long trip, but your mother confided to my mother that you had gone away. She said your mother cried and would only say she missed you so much."

He looked Jakobi in the eyes. Shaking his head, he asked, "Why don't you return home, Jakobi?"

The wagon Abijah rode in had slowed down so he gave a signal to advise the others to go on ahead and that he would catch up with them in town.

As the men rode on, he put his arm across Jakobi's shoulders and asked, "Why did you leave, Jakobi? Why did you leave home and family? Life simply could not have been that bad!"

Needing to unburden himself, Jakobi slowly poured out his story. "I was a fool, Abijah. I wanted to be just like you – being independent, having my friends over, able to host parties and serve fine wines, to do as I pleased."

His friend drew back and shouted, "Whaattttt? What are you saying, Jakobi?" He laughed so hard he could feel hiccups rising in his chest and throat as he bent over double. Jakobi looked at him in amazement. Eventually, he gurgled and, with tears in his eyes, gave a wide smile. He took his sleeve and wiped his eyes.

"I am not independent, my friend! I still have to answer to my father and mother. In fact, my mother just had another talk with me to find a nice woman to marry – one of many talks lately. I know I have reached the age where I know I should plan for some stability, a wife, and perhaps children. I already have a place of my own. But I also know I'm not quite ready for such things."

"I look at my brother, Joash, who has a beautiful wife and daughter and, just recently, a brand new son, and he seems to be at peace. That's what I really want, but unfortunately I have not settled on the right girl as yet. My mother has started the ordeal of introducing me to what seems to be all the girls in the area. They have all been lovely to look at, but some seem to have very little hay in the loft, if you understand what I mean." Abijah smiled at his little joke.

"Now your sister, Salome, is very beautiful Jakobi. Someone of her beauty, intelligence, wit and personality would make a wonderful wife, but still I would be waiting in line behind countless other suitors. Your father has not made a decision on whom he would like as a son-in-law. She treats me nicely enough so I know she is not adverse to my company, but getting past your father and Eliakim has come to be a greater obstacle than you would be if you were home."

"My funds have grown, but not enough to keep a home and family as my father has kept Ramani and me. My brother, Joash is doing very well. He and your brother, Eliakim, use the same advisors set up by our fathers. One gets used to the good life and I would never want to put my family or myself in a position of poverty."

"Funds?" questioned Jakobi, "what do you mean by your 'funds have grown'?" Abijah stared at him in surprise.

"How do you think I'm able to do what I do? My father decided to increase my allowance and gave me money to invest. He called it my starter fund. Over a year's time, I saved the better portion of my allowance and took part of it to purchase some property, a few servants, and some sheep, but I still continued my parties. Of course, not as often as before because I think I'm starting to get away from my wild life, as my mother calls it."

"Yahweh has blessed me to have productive herds and they have multiplied twice in the three years I have raised them. I even have cattle, sheep, and goats and have donated some to the synagogue for sacrifice. My crops sold very well and I have purchased more land. It is my plan to double my grain next year on some of the property I have just recently purchased."

"In fact, my friend, the property I now live on was purchased by me from an older man who was moving to join his daughter and son-in-law who live far away. His wife died and he was going to move closer to his only daughter. I bought it for a song and it needed very little renovation. That's not the same house where you attended my parties before you left home. It is much bigger and does not belong to my parents, but to me.

"My sister. Ramani – as you might remember, she had a crush on you a long time ago – helped me furnish it with curtains, tables, and those womanly little touches and knickknacks; and I have recently purchased new furniture through the traders. It looks even nicer than my old place since you were last there. When you get back, make a point of dropping by to see what I've done with it!" Abijah gave a wide grin as he proudly stuck his chest out.

Jakobi could not believe what he was hearing as Abijah proudly explained his investments.

"You had funds to invest?" He was aghast. Abijah continued smiling and nodded in the affirmative.

"The two men I am traveling with are my advisors. My father introduced me to them a few years ago and they have helped me to make wise decisions. In fact, we are returning from looking at special fig trees and olive groves. I wish to purchase a few to have planted on my newly purchased properties."

"I even talked to your sister-in-law, Hannah, who explained the value of growing my own olives from the trees I plan to purchase. Did you know she has her own revenue? Your brother allowed her to hire her own servants and they make money from the oil they sell. She has such a business head."

"I have just completed the purchases today and a few of my servants will return with larger wagons later in the week to pick them up."

"As you know, like you, I am the second son, and it is important that I look out for myself as my inheritance will not be as great as Joash's. And, if I say so myself, I am doing quite well."

"Yahweh has bestowed on me His favor. I may not become as well-to-do as my brother, but I will certainly not be poor either. When I have my children, I want my sons to be able to inherit property, herds and goods from me; and if I have girls, they will be sent off to their marriages with a good dowry. If I am blessed to have five sons, none of them need be ashamed of their inheritance."

At the mention of future children, Abijah gave a large grin.

"I have been attending the synagogue services a lot more often because I now believe that if it wasn't for Yahweh nothing that I've done so far will count."

"This past year I was able to have my reapers leave my fields open to many gleaners. They were able to share in my bounty as well. When I was a child, I always saw how my father allowed the gleaners to gather behind his reapers every year as they harvested his crops. When he saw men gathering the chaff along with the wheat, he would go to them and teach them how to effectively glean."

"He has always said if I wanted to be blessed, I should do the same and look out for those who have nothing. So for the last few years I have done so and my fields have been flourishing, even through the famine. Yahweh is good!"

He put one of his hands to his forehead in thought. "You know, Jakobi, for years I did not know I was very selfish. I had a little land, a few servants, had my parties and enjoyed my friends, but soon it seemed as if everyone who enjoyed my bounty reaped a benefit, but I was still unfulfilled. Since I have been more giving toward others, I now seem to be enjoying life more fully."

Jakobi was very surprised. As he listened to Abijah, he could see where he had gone wrong. His friend continued talking about how the Lord had blessed him. He could not say anything for he knew that if he had listened to his father and brother, things would be much different for him. He would not be working with pigs in a foreign land for a non-Jew.

Abijah jumped from the wagon as Jakobi turned the cart and pulled toward the lane to retrieve the grain for which he was sent.

"Wait, Abijah! Did you say that Ramani used to have a crush on me? Is that true?"

"Sure. She told me that a long time ago, but was always uneasy around some of my friends. Then she never mentioned it again. She used to walk through the house with refreshments when my friends visited, but soon stopped and left the trays of food on a table for me to take to them. I realized then that she did not like the looks my friends were giving her. I'm surprised you never noticed that she no longer walked through with the food."

Jakobi knew it was because of Abijah's friends and his own lifestyle. He thought of something his father had once said to him: 'Your activities of the past can ruin your future." He shook his head as he noticed Abijah was still talking to him.

"What should I tell your parents when I return home, Jakobi? I know they would hate to see you looking as sparse as you do and your clothes with the smell of swine on them."

Jakobi wanted to say that Abijah should tell his family nothing, but then thought about it and said, "Tell them you saw me and I looked to be in good health — especially say this to my mother. That's all they need to know – not that I am a caretaker of swine and that my body reeks of their smell. Please do that for me."

Abijah nodded his head, then turned toward a street of vendors where he could see his men of business waiting.

"I will be kind," he quietly said. "Should you ever return home, please look me up. You have a great family, a mother who misses you, a father who wanted only the best for you, and sisters who looked up to you. Your brother, Eliakim, told me it seems as if the life has gone out of his family. Your family is sad without you. That's all I'm going to say -- for your life is your own. You've proven to your family that you are your own man."

His friend started down the street as Jakobi began to turn the wagon onto a well-worn road to head toward his original destination. But Abijah himself turned around and looked Jakobi straight in the face.

"I have one last thing to tell you," he shouted, "and it is this: 'Jakobi, go home! Go home, my friend, go home to your family!'"

That said, Abijah turned and continued on his way to meet his waiting advisors.

12

Jakobi once again clicked his tongue to move the donkeys forward and began to mull over the information Abijah had just given him. He could see where his mistakes lay in not listening to his father and brother. Eliakim had tried to advise him about using his allowance to do things other than party with his friends. He realized how he could have saved some of his money, invested wisely, increased his allowance through working with the same advisors Eliakim worked with.

And Ramani! He never knew she paid any attention to him. She probably only saw a friend of her brother who partied and drank until daybreak. He thought about it and it came to him that he had never seen Abijah drunk. He drank very little wine and was always in control, although his friends, including himself, drank until they could drink no more.

How much money had he personally squandered since he began receiving an allowance from his father? He spent even more when his father raised his allowance. He should have used his money more to his advantage.

His elder brother did not seem to use all the money his father gave him, but was able to purchase sheep, cattle and chickens for a small farm he visited on the outskirts. Could that small farm be the result of his own investments? He had never asked Eliakim about the small farm and knew he still owned it. Eliakim's eldest son went there each week and he realized that perhaps his nephews may be working the farm for their dad. Now that he looked back, he could see that Eliakim used his business head even in his youth.

Two men always came twice a month to talk with his father and then with his brother; Jakobi now believed they were his father's and Eliakim's business advisors.

How does one become an advisor, he wondered. Probably by making good investments and passing along such knowledge to others. Such investments gave the person a good reputation. Father always gave good advice to relatives and friends and would possibly make a great advisor.

It did not take an idiot to see that his so-called unscrupulous advisor, Ezzidin, had no real training. He was just a man who used others' money to his advantage.

Why did he not pay more attention? He also knew his father knew other investors who had, perhaps, helped in Eliakim's business decisions. He knew his father had tried to help him, but he had ignored his advice. This was only a supposition, but the more he thought about it, he believed he may be correct.

13

Jakobi was so busy thinking, he almost missed turning down the dirt road to the place where he would pick up the grain. He slowly turned the donkeys around and headed in the right direction.

As he reached the market area, he saw foreign traders approaching. Since he was not familiar with traders from other nations, he tried to guess where they were from by their clothing. He also realized the material they wore was not what traders normally wore because of their rich colors and fine material.

Their clothing reminded him of what he used to wear before he got into dire straits and realized they were probably some of the traders who sold such clothing to his parents. In order to survive, he had to sell his beautiful robes and knew he did not receive adequate money for their value.

Strange, he had never thought about where his clothes came from or what they cost — only that such articles were always in his closet to wear whenever and wherever he pleased. His mother always made sure the family's closets had robes, veils, sandals and scarves for any occasion and her husband and children were able to dress in rich-looking clothing whenever they went away from home. He once had different types of clothing for work, synagogue, and even to wear to his many parties.

He looked down at his torn and ragged clothes and the fact that he had no sandals on his feet. Ah, he thought; only the very lowest servants in his father's house did not have sandals. They were useless in the fields and most of the servants did not find them comfortable since they had not been raised wearing them. The household servants were given sandals, but most times they went barefoot unless his parents entertained.

There were four traders in the small cart with some of their wares inside the cart as well as hanging on the sides. As they passed, he saw beautiful pottery, scarves, colored cloth, and beautifully-made sandals.

The thin man driving the cart, wearing bright blue colors, smiled at him, showing uneven teeth as he chewed on a small stick. Beside him sat a dark-skinned man with a multi-colored turban beating a drum to draw attention to their wares. Jakobi watched as the town's women hailed the cart to look over their wares.

Two young girls who looked to be a little older than the age of his sisters, Salome and Rachel, were fingering a fine scarf as the older girl put it next to her chest. The younger one was nodding her head as if she agreed with the colors. There was an older woman standing to the side of the girls watching. He believed she may be their mother or a beloved servant who chaperoned them.

Jakobi knew if the scarf was purchased it would look beautiful on either one of them. Jakobi shook his head to clear such thoughts as he turned away.

The scene made him homesick for his mother and sisters.

A caravan of camels, donkeys and people soon blocked his view as he traveled onward.

This was all Abijah's fault, he decided. It started with his friend mentioning his home and family and how much they missed him. Then the traders with their wares, sellers of clothing, sandals and scarves, and now the two girls. God, he missed his family, even his father.

14

He soon reached his destination, transacted Emad-Shevets' business with the merchant and helped put the grain into the cart. At least the merchant was honest, for he returned some of the coins to him saying Jakobi had given him too much money.

As he lifted himself back into the wagon, he saw some of his old Samaritan friends in a wagon and smiled as they turned their backs on him as if they'd never met him. He thought about yelling loudly to them by calling their names, but decided against it. If one does not want to be noticed, then one should not be noticed. He clicked his tongue to move the donkeys forward and headed back to Emad-Shevets and his pigs.

Jakobi turned in at the gate to Emad-Shevets' holdings and came to a stop at the stable doors. Holding the reins to the donkeys, he waited as three servants emerged from the back of the building to help take the grain off the wagon and place the bags inside the stables. Emad-Shevets came out of his house and checked the bags as the men unloaded the merchandise. He smiled when Jakobi returned the unused money to him.

Turning the animals around, he headed toward the north pasture, parked the wagon and took the equipment and reins off the pair to release them. He watched as the two donkeys walked side by side to the pasture where a few horses were grazing. There were a few bushes and small trees near a small watering hole that was used by the donkeys, and other farm animals.

Jakobi could swear he saw a slight movement behind the bushes. As he blinked, the movement was no longer there. Shrugging his shoulders, he blinked a few more times as he walked, thinking the sun was playing tricks with his eyes.

"I must be very tired," he thought. "I could swear I saw a man slightly hidden near the pool's greenery." Shaking his head, he turned toward the pig styes.

Dragging his feet, he slowly made his way to an area near the pigs and went to the back of the building. It was time for the evening meal and he was hungry. He smelled something cooking and wondered what the cook was fixing for the evening meal for the aroma was not very pleasant.

The smell brought to mind the delicious odors that would always greet him when he was living at home. His mother, sisters, and the servants in the kitchen always collaborated together to plan the daily meals for the family.

While they employed many servants, Zyama herself always set up menus for the week. Many times she would help in the kitchen by cutting up vegetables and slicing delicious fruit for she enjoyed working with the kitchen servants. She made sure his sisters knew how to cook, clean, and run a household.

Zyama was a thrifty woman and a great cook herself, for she was raised to do household chores. Her mother made sure she was able to do such duties so that when she married, her husband would know his household was in capable hands.

A few years ago, Zyama had a horrible cold and his sister, Salome, took over the household duties. Although she was young, he remembered everything ran as smoothly as when his mother was in charge. Salome would make a wonderful wife for some lucky man and she was beautiful as well as very intelligent.

Jakobi laughed at himself. He made a point of never introducing her to his friends. It did not bother him to hang out with his friends but he realized early as Salome began to mature that he did not want any of them to become his brother-in-law. It really didn't bother him too much because he knew Matthan would never strike a betrothal alliance with any suitor for the hands of his two beloved daughters.

Yes, he knew his father and Abijah's father were cut from the same cloth!

He had to stop thinking of his sisters for once again Jakobi became very sad, so he shook his head and continued toward the eating area.

15

Eliakim, his wife Hannah, and his mother, Zyama were walking through the center of town to the marketplace when he saw Abijah and his mother heading the same way. As both families approached, the women stopped to chat. Zyama, Hannah and Nihomi exchanged news of their families as Eliakim spoke with Abijah.

The two men discussed their crops and the upcoming harvest. Abijah was only too happy to report his elation at the profit made from this year's crop. Eliakim said he wished his brother was able to see the progress Abijah had made in his land purchases and produce. When Abijah averted his eyes, Eliakim discerned that his brother's friend had made contact with Jakobi. He knew without a doubt that Abijah had information on his brother and his heart began to race.

Eliakim lowered his voice as he put his arm around Abijah's shoulders and led him a few feet away from the women.

"You've seen Jakobi, haven't you?" Abijah eyes blinked but said nothing. Eliakim persisted, "You know where he is, don't you?"

Abijah put his head down and tried to change the subject but Eliakim was persistent. Inwardly he groaned. He had made a promise to Jakobi.

"Tell me!" Eliakim knew without a doubt that Abijah knew where his brother had settled and how he was faring. He squeezed Abijah's shoulders and made contact with his eyes. "Tell me, Abijah! Tell me!"

Although he had his head down, Abijah remembered that Jakobi made him promise that he would not tell his friend's family about his true situation. However, Jakobi never said he was not to discuss his lifestyle with Jakobi's brother. With his mind working quickly, he tried to remember exactly what Jakobi told him to tell his family.

"Your brother is doing well and seems to be in good health," was his mumbled reply. "I did not have a long conversation with him but I understand he is working on a prosperous farm. That's really all I can tell you."

Abijah kept his head lowered, but blushed furiously. Eliakim knew there was more Abijah could tell him, but decided to quit prompting him for he could see he would receive no further information from his brother's friend. After all, Abijah had known Jakobi since childhood and he was aware that a good friend would keep another's secrets. Who knew what his brother wanted the family to actually know about his situation?

"Thank you, Abijah," he sighed in relief, "I will not push you further but you have set my mind at rest. At least Jakobi is alive and well. My parents mourn him as if he is dead. You'd think they only had one child — Jakobi! The information you gave me is more than we've heard these few years. I will not push you for more because I know you are loyal to your friend."

Gratefully, Abijah nodded his head as the two turned toward the women, who were still carrying on a casual conversation.

The men slowly sauntered toward the women. Eliakim smiled at Abijah and clapped him on his shoulders before they approached.

"Thank you again, my friend; I really appreciate even that bit of information."

Abijah was relieved that there would be no more questions this day. He thought of Jakobi as his friend and had promised to only give limited information to Jakobi's family.

He stopped walking, placed his hand on Eliakim's shoulder as he looked into his eyes. "I was told to tell your mother, if I was asked, that he is alive and well, so that is what I am telling you to tell her. Please do that for me."

Eliakim nodded and smiled as he and Abijah carried on a normal conversation as they approached the chatting women. He began to pick at fruit that was on display on a trader's fruit and vegetable cart, and chose a bunch of dates.

It did not escape Hannah's notice that her normally quiet and aloof husband seemed to be very talkative with Abijah.

Without asking her husband, Hannah knew Abijah possibly had information concerning the whereabouts of Jakobi. She knew Eliakim worried about his younger brother as much as his mother, but kept his feelings bottled up.

Hannah loved Eliakim and was aware he believed his parents sometimes treated him as a second son, instead of the oldest. Since his brother left, their thoughts were always on Jakobi and his whereabouts. She did not say anything to her husband, yet knew that when he was ready, he would confide in her.

Quickly she turned her thoughts back to the other women's conversation and joined in.

16

As they reached the women, Eliakim changed the subject to discuss the sale of cattle which was coming up in a few days.

"You men," quipped Abijah's mother, Nihomi. "All you talk about are cattle, sheep and crops. Eliakim, cannot you change the subject and talk to my son as to how he should start giving thought to finding a good wife? Eliakim, tell him how happy you and Hannah are in your marriage."

Hannah lowered her head and gave a slight blush. Eliakim smiled as he watched her and lightly touched her arm.

Zyama noticed the movement and smiled. She was pleased her eldest son and his wife were happy. They had two young sons, both of whom were the spitting image of their father and were hard workers. Soon the eldest would celebrate his bar mitzvah.

Already her grandson has mentioned to her a few of the young ladies from prominent families in the area whose fathers, she was sure, would be happy to set up betrothal contracts.

Yes, Zyama was pleased with her eldest son and his family. Eliakim had made good choices.

If only, if only, she thought, she could hear news of Jakobi. Her husband had told her to not mourn for their younger son. She was not in mourning, she had admitted to him, because then she would admit he may have died and that is not what she wished. She just wanted to hear news of him; to know that he was alive and well; to be able to see him once again.

Oh, to have him home once more!

She knew she would not be feeling this way if Jakobi had married a nice your woman and lived in another village, but that was not the case. At least in another village, she might be able to see him or he could easily visit the family. Such was not to be.

"Now Mother," Abijah smiled, "perhaps it will happen soon. I have set my eyes on one beautiful girl, but father and I have not spoken with the family as yet."

He shifted his eyes over to Eliakim, who started to look questioningly at him. Suddenly it dawned on him that Abijah was referring to one of his sisters. It had to be Salome who was closest to Abijah's age. He smiled to himself.

They reached the last trader's wagon and the women began fingering the brightly colored materials. There were beautiful scarves flapping in the slight breeze and Hannah held one against her hip and commented to her mother-in-law on its colors and rich texture.

The trader's partner came around the cart toward the group of women and quickly began expounding on the colors and how the scarf could be used as a girdle or around Hannah's neck and head. He and the first trader began pulling scarves off their wagon, competing for a sale.

The first one began flattering Hannah and showing how another scarf of subdued colors would enhance her beautiful eyes and would look marvelous on her. Hannah looked longingly at the scarf, but shook her head as she quietly explained she was not shopping for a new scarf at the present time. She stepped back and allowed the other two women to finger more scarves.

Eliakim smiled and gave a quiet signal to the trader who quickly came to his side. He surreptitiously handed the trader a few coins. The happy trader's eyes widened as he looked at the coins and wrapped the scarf Hannah had just looked at and added another colorful one to the sale, for he realized the man was being generous. The first scarf was the one Hannah had picked up, but slowly placed back on the trader's pile of material. He quietly wrapped both scarves, placed them in a small thin burlap bag and handed the bag to Eliakim, who had his back to his wife.

Abijah watched the entire scenario and smiled. Yes, Eliakim was a good husband and he could see that Eliakim would be giving the scarves to his wife as a surprise when they reached their home.

That was the type of marriage he wanted.

17

Upon his arrival to the farm, Jakobi picked up his pottery bowl and spoon-like utensil and headed toward the large cooking area. Seeing what was in the pot made him nauseous. Inside was a type of concoction that somewhat resembled something the pigs ate. Whatever it was had been thrown into the pot and was boiling vigorously.

As the grayish concoction bubbled over the heat, he set his bowl and utensil aside and left the mealroom. Hungry as he was, he could not bring himself to eat the food. Lately the food was getting worse. He had been with Emad-Shevets long enough to know that his employer, although quite well-to-do, was not going to spend additional funds to feed his workers adequate meals.

He watched the other servants as the concoction was spooned into their bowls and realized they were so used to this type of food that their stomachs no longer quaked.

18

As the years continued to fly by, Jakobi was becoming more and more disgruntled with his lot in life. He hated the pigs, he hated the farm, he hated Emad-Shevets and he hated Emad-Shevets' ugly daughter. He could only blame himself. No one placed this burden on him — he did it to himself.

"Why, oh why," he berated himself. "Why did I make the decision to leave home and family? What good did it do me to leave a life as befitting a man of my stature to come to this area just to raise and care for pigs!"

While sitting on the fence watching the sows wallow in the mud with their newborn piglets, out of the corner of his right eye he watched the approach of Hoshi. He also noted a bald head with beady eyes staring at Hoshi from behind. Could the unknown person be the same person he thought he saw near the donkey's watering hole?

Hoshi must have felt eyes upon her, for she quickly turned her head to see if someone was behind her, but the man had disappeared from view.

As Jakobi groaned inwardly at her approach, he raised one of his eyebrows and contemplated jumping off the fence railing and heading for the relief area.

Too late, she was in front of him smiling coquettishly.

"My father wishes to speak with you," she loudly informed him as her eyes slid over his slim frame. "He is waiting for you in the front of the house."

After delivering her message, she continued to stand in front of him while still looking him over.

Jakobi slowly slid to the ground without responding and quickly headed toward the house with long strides. Hoshi began walking faster in order to keep up with him.

"I know how to get to the house," he flatly growled and continued walking. She stopped at the sound of his voice and changed direction.

Jakobi almost felt sorry for her, but he did not want to be bothered with the Canaanite daughter of his employer. He did not really like the spoiled, petulant girl and he knew he did not want to deal with her in any way. She would be the type to cry foul and land him in loads of trouble. Her walk was suggestive of her character and he knew she should not be near the outdoor servants, especially near the pigs.

As he walked toward the main house, he met up with other men who also worked with the pigs, who had also been summoned and the three walked forward as they could see their master standing in front of the building.

At that moment, a young male servant rushed toward him and apologetically said he was glad to see him because he was to have delivered a message to Jakobi informing him of Emad-Shevets' summons.

"I'm sorry I was late, but I had two duties to perform and could not get to you soon enough. I'm glad the other men informed you." The man looked somewhat contrite, but Jakobi waved him off.

"Don't worry about it," he said as he continued walking with the other workers.

Ah, hah! Jakobi thought. Here was the true messenger who was to have delivered the summons, not Hoshi. It seems Hoshi took it upon herself to deliver the message.

Emad-Shevets stood near the doorway and watched as his daughter tried to follow Jakobi, hesitated and then turned toward the stables. He knew she had set her eyes on the Jew and did not approve, but thankfully saw that Jakobi was handling the problem on his own. Jakobi was too poor for his taste as well as being a Jew; and besides, he had a very well-to-do prospect in mind for his daughter.

As the men approached him, Emad-Shevets continued to study Jakobi. He had to admit that although the Jew had lost some weight since he first came to work for him, yet, there was muscle on his thin frame. He was a handsome young man and a good worker, but knew he had to be in dire straits in order to work with swine. He smiled as he thought to himself how Jews and swine were not compatible.

Jakobi stood in front of him and said, "I understand you wanted to see us." Etufi and the three other servants nodded their heads acknowledging that they were also informed.

"Yes, I wanted you all to know that I have another shipment of pigs to be delivered tomorrow. Business is good so plan to be at the back when the carts arrive to make sure they are put in the new styes the men are setting up. Some had given birth over a few months ago and I want the piglets separated from their sows. See to it that it is done quickly so we won't hear a lot of noise all night. Those piglets get upset when they're separated from their mamas. They should already be weaned so you can give them small amounts of grain and mash."

That said, he turned and headed toward the back of the house.

Jakobi looked at the other pig workers and as they looked at each other, none said anything but turned and headed back toward the styes.

Jakobi had watched the arrival of the wood for the new styes and watched as a group of servants began setting them up. The area that was used for the new rails let him know that a great deal more pigs would be put in them. He groaned just thinking about more of those stinking, ugly pigs arriving tomorrow.

19

Jakobi awakened early the next morning. Even though he was always up before the sun rose, he could see that it was still the middle of the night. He sat up on his pallet and considered his life once again. As the years passed, he began to think more and more about home: his father, his brother, sisters, and most of all, his mother. Because of his hasty decision-making all he had were the memories of his last goodbyes.

He then thought of his father and how he had tried to talk him into staying. He had been willing to find advisors for him to learn to make good investments. He made the same offer for Eliakim and it seems his brother had listened to every one of them.

Whenever his father went on business trips he would always hug his wife and each of his children because, as he said, "you never know which time will be the last. It is always a blessing to leave with love in good stead and know that when you return love awaits you. To leave with love in your heart is a blessing, and to return and know that love awaits you when you return is another blessing," Matthan always said.

Jakobi did not hug his father when he departed from home. He had gotten up early, finished packing, and left the homestead in order to avoid having to see his family.

He really loved his father, but by not hugging him on his way out, he missed out on the blessing.

Jakobi sniffled a few seconds and then began to cry. Eventually, he began to silently sob, trying not to awaken the other servants in the sleeping room.

The barnlike structure was not a private bedroom and it was all he could do to hold his sorrow inside. He lay back down and drew his tattered blanket under his chin.

One of the servants, Etufi, heard him and kept his thoughts to himself. He knew the Jewish man did not like working with the pigs and the food was not to his liking. Not a man to pry, he rolled over on his own pallet and closed his eyes.

Within a short time, through the opening of a small window, Jakobi could see the sun coming over the hills, heading toward sunrise. He stayed on his pallet and watched the sun rise over the far hills with its yellow, orange and red coloring. When he heard the other men stirring, he got up and headed for the relief area.

As he headed behind the barn, he thought he saw an unfamiliar man heading away from the relief area. He had been working with the pigs for some time and knew most of the servants. Perhaps the man was a new servant.

Probably lower paid than he and the others, he thought. Yet, the man seemed to be trying to hide from his sight. Is this the same man he had been glimpsing off and on?

Jakobi quickened his steps to try to see the man's face, but the man was much quicker. When he reached the relief area, there was no sign of him.

He knew his eyes were not playing tricks on him, but it seemed strange that the man seemed to avoid the servants. Guron and Ranal caught up with him and all headed in the same direction while laughing and telling jokes.

20

The rain was slowly falling in a drizzle over the countryside. Matthan had decided earlier that morning it was time to check on his herds of sheep. Although it was not shearing time, he could see that many needed to have their fur cut low because the fur seemed to be slowing them down. But, within a few hours, the rain had started. Of course his crops and animals could use the rain, for the heat had been unbearable for some time. First the heat, then the famine in late spring, and now the unceasing rain. Odd weather for this time of the year.

The shepherds had gone into their tents to cook and eat their midday meal and the cattle and sheep herds had grouped together, putting their heads down.

He looked his land over and praised Yahweh for the abundance of his possessions. He was proud of Eliakim for he had made suggestions to him of rotating his crops and moving the sheep to higher ground. His son's ideas had been a blessing and he had quickly observed the large crop of grain and knew with the rain the harvest would be plentiful.

Matthan knew it was Eliakim's ideas which had increased his and Hannah's revenue. He was very pleased that their marriage was a love match and they seemed to work well together. Hannah's math skills and money management had made an abundant growth for both families. Their sons seemed to take after their parents, not only in looks, but also in intellect.

If only he knew what was happening with his other son. Jakobi was highly educated, so it wasn't as if he could not write to his family. If not to him, at least write to his mother.

Zyama said she knew in her heart that her youngest son was alive, but what of his condition? Was Jakobi eating correctly? In what area was he living? Was he someplace friendly -- she knew Jews were not always accepted in some areas.

Matthan had been told by Eliakim that Abijah had seen Jakobi and that his report to him was that his brother was "doing well."

Not that he did not believe Abijah, for he knew his son would have told Abijah what words he should report back to his family. He appreciated his son's friend for giving them even that little bit of information, but thought it best to tell his wife nothing. She would go to Abijah's mother and try to squeeze information out of her; yet Abijah may not have told his own mother anything and she may not have any information to give to Zyama. This would only make his wife yearn even more for Jakobi than what she felt now.

Abijah did not tell Eliakim where he met with his son, or what area or town he may be living in. His only information was that Abijah ran into him while making a purchase in one of the many marketplaces he had visited.

Matthan put his finger to the side of his head and thought of how he once wanted independence from his father when he was around the age of 16 or 17. He was a second son and saw the favor given to the eldest. His father ruled his family with an iron hand. He knew if he had decided to leave home, he would never have asked for his part of the inheritance. Was he ever strict with his sons? Did Eliakim ever wish to leave when he was younger?

His relationship with Eliakim was different from his relationship with Jakobi. Eliakim was his son and Jakobi was his mother's son. He never had a problem from his firstborn, but the problems he had with Jakobi were handled more leniently because Zyama always made excuses for him. Jakobi was spoiled and that was his own fault. He showed love to them both, but not in the same manner.

He thought of his girls. Salome, the elder, was beautiful, intelligent, and obedient. Rachel, the youngest, was also beautiful and intelligent; she was always playful, and enjoyed life. She and Salome were loving sisters and he knew Salome made sure her little sister was taught how to act like a young lady and kept her in line. Both never gave him a moment's problem. Rachel's beauty was not in the same category as her sister, for she was the image of his wife. Did he ever show more love to the younger than he showed to the elder because she was the baby?

Was there a noticeable distinction of his love between his four children? He loved them all; but was his family a Jacob and Joseph story? Jacob had many children — yet showed more attention to Joseph than to the others. Could any man show the same amount or type of love to all of his children?

That was something to ponder for another time. There was work to be done and standing around questioning himself would not get any work completed or settle the problem.

He gave a huge sigh and headed toward the house to discuss some matters with Gupta.

21

The new pigs were to arrive directly after the so-called morning meal. He looked in his bowl and saw it was more gray pig slop. Jakobi ate just enough of the meal to satisfy his hunger since he did not eat the previous night, but did not finish it.

"Why am I eating this stuff?" he asked himself. "My father would never serve his own servants this type of meal. Why, even the lowliest workers eat better food than this."

He headed for the main pig sty and not long after the carts arrived bringing the new pigs and their piglets. Emad-Shevets came outside and for a short time watched them being unloaded and soon left. Jakobi placed grain and water in the troughs and noticed how nice the grain and mash looked versus what he had to eat that morning.

Jakobi and the other servants first separated the sows and boars and herded them toward the old styes. They had previously picked up the squealing piglets that were already in the old styes and placed them with the new piglets that had just arrived.

He and the other servants had to chase a few of the piglets in order to transfer them. As they ran from the men, it soon became a game to the piglets and the servants laughed at their clumsiness while trying to catch them. The little ones were very slippery and as they caught them, some tried kicking their back legs to be released. The men knew this would happen and some held them upside down by their legs as they carried them to the new styes.

As the men separated the new piglets, all of the pigs began screaming. The mamas were screaming and grunting 'bring back my babies' and the youngsters were screaming 'we want our mamas.'

"How sad," Jakobi morosely thought. "I want my mama, too!"

As he lined up behind the other servants for the evening meal, he looked in the large pot as the porridge boiled gray and lumpy and thought about the pig's food. At least the animals' food had color; this bubbly stuff was grayish-brown and very, very lumpy.

Jakobi jerked his head back. He was surprised at his thoughts. It's a sorry thought that the pigs' food was certainly starting to look better than what was in the pot. If his thoughts continued along this vein, he would soon start wallowing in the mud and making grunting noises. Such thoughts had to be the last straw!

Slowly he placed the gourd inside the pot and scooped out a few spoonsful of the gray matter and grabbed a few small pieces of the hard brown bread. Once again, he ate just enough to keep his stomach from growling and left the room.

Another servant, Etufi, followed Jakobi and caught up with him. Jakobi turned his head and smiled at him, but could see Etufi had something on his mind.

"Jakobi," he began, "have you noticed someone watching the house lately?"

Jakobi jerked his head toward the other man. "Yes, but I thought it was my eyes. I've seen him a few times, including this morning. If you've seen him too, then I am not hallucinating!"

Etufi matched his steps to Jakobi's. "I don't believe he's just watching the house, but is more likely watching Hoshi. Whenever Hoshi is outside, he seems to always be around."

"Yes, but I don't think Hoshi knows him or she would know of his presence and possibly say something to him. I also don't think Emad-Shevets knows the man either or he would not be sneaking around."

Etufi shuffled his feet and looked around the yard. "This man is not a suitor because I've watched all the suitors and they are younger, somewhat well-to-do and are from around this area."

Once again Jakobi was aghast, but happy he had never said anything against Hoshi around his fellow servants, for he never thought about Etufi or any of them having feelings for her. He stared at his fellow worker.

"You have feelings for Hoshi? Enough feelings to know all of her suitors?"

Shame-faced Etufi put his head down. Jakobi could see the flush on his face when he finally raised his head and smiled at him.

No answer.

Keeping in step the two men walked slowly toward the pig styes to check on the pigs and make sure the wood was still in place. Fixing a few planks to make sure the sows did not try to escape, they later joined the other workers and headed toward their sleeping area.

Etufi glanced sideways at Jakobi and it was clear Etufi did not want the others to know of his feelings for Hoshi. Jakobi looked back and gave a slow wink to his friend, who was satisfied that his secret was safe.

22

Hoshi sat on a small stool by the tool shed and watched the male servants return from their evening meal and head toward their various work areas. The men who were over the pigs were the last to arrive.

It was late and the sun was slowly setting. She knew the men would not be overly busy because there was little they could do as night fell. Most of the time, they hung around the pig styes and talked with each other.

Etufi watched her as she sat and watched each of the men returning from their meals. He knew there was no hope for him as he would never be one of her suitors. He tried to get her attention many times, but she ignored him and only watched Jakobi. He noticed Jakobi did not like the attention she gave to him and was pleased.

Whenever Hoshi tried to get his attention, the Jew would either change direction, or ignore her presence. Etufi felt he had a better chance with the girl than Jakobi. Her father would never sanction any type of relationship for his daughter with a Jew.

He was from Tyre, and possessed more than a little money through inheritance. His father felt it was only right that he try to earn money to help set up his own household and not use his inheritance until he was older. Etufi decided that any money he was able to earn would be saved to help purchase land and animals. Of course, the woman he married would have some type of dowry to bring to the marriage. He was also aware that he was more than able to provide for a wife and, hopefully later, children.

Although he set his heart on Hoshi, he knew he would have to look to his own kind for a wife. He had no prospects in the areas of Canaan or Samaria and did not find their women very comely. The women from his village had beauty and would welcome marriage to him, but he felt it didn't hurt to look around. It was almost time for him to return to his own area for he was getting older and, more and more, thought of a home of his own.

Yet, there was something sensuous about Hoshi. She was not beautiful, but he knew she was ready to marry from the way she swayed her hips and constantly approached the men in the fields and around the household. She had learned the art of seduction, but being young did not yet know how she affected the male species.

He was not the first servant to notice this for the men were wont to discuss Hoshi as they worked. The only thing that stopped them from approaching her was Emad-Shevets. He was a big man and strong. A man's neck could be crushed in less than two seconds by Hoshi's father if any one of them was seen too close to his only daughter.

When Etufi first arrived to work with the pigs, he, as well as other new servants, was given the rules by Emad-Shevets, and rule number one was to never, ever be near his daughter – not to talk to her or be alone with her. All the male servants complied with this rule.

There were rumors concerning previous male servants approaching Hoshi and being fired by her father. Rumor had it that one servant tried to talk to her and he was no longer seen again. Was he fired or buried under a pig stye or in one of Emad-Shevets fields?

Although Etufi always made a point of being where he could watch her, he never tried to get too close.

Etufi 's family was not a poor one according to the standards of Tyre, but he was not of the same nationality as Hoshi's family. His father wanted him to experience the outside world and earn his own money. The only one to hire him in this area was Emad-Shevets and since there were no other positions available, he accepted the low wages that were offered.

He knew Hoshi's father was angling for bigger fish, and that did not include a foreigner who was a servant. Emad-Shevets didn't question the servants' backgrounds or why they wished to work. He accepted them as servants for he had need of workers. Today, Etufi worked at the new pig styes alongside Jakobi and three other servants.

As Hoshi continued her trek through the farmyard, all stopped to watch. Although they knew Hoshi walked in front of them to get their attention, none said anything to the others.

Finally Jakobi began to chuckle, then Etufi joined in and finally all of the men began to laugh loudly. Hoshi saw them bent over laughing while holding their sides and became irate. She watched them for a short time and haughtily hastened toward the house.

Locating her mother in the sewing room, she sat down and tearfully told her mother about those horrible pig servants.

23

The next morning Emad-Shevets required all of the male servants from the pig styes to report quickly to him. Each knew Emad-Shevets was angry when they arrived in front of the house. He was huffing and puffing and his face had turned a bluish purple color.

As they stood in front of him, their employer began screaming at them to leave his daughter alone.

"I do not like to see my daughter with red-rimmed eyes from crying. You are **not** to be around my daughter at all! You all know the consequences of that!"

He sputtered for another few minutes and paused to catch his breath. As the men nodded their heads, they watched as his face changed colors and slowly went back to his florid pink. All knew Emad-Shevets loved his daughter deeply and quietly listened to his ranting.

Finally, when they could get a word in, Etufi stepped forward and calmly explained, "My lord, none of us goes near your daughter and we do not approach the house unless summoned by you."

"However, we suggest it would be wise for you to inform your daughter that the pig styes are not to be approached without a chaperone or servant."

Although he was flushed a deep pink, Emad-Shevets looked shocked. "What? What are you saying? My daughter goes near the pigs? That cannot be – for she hates pigs!"

"That may be so," answered another servant named Ranal, "but she is always in the area near the styes. We do not even speak with her because of your command. She sometimes sits on the fence and tries to talk to us. We never answer her. There are even times she will follow us as we work. As Etufi has said, we do not have anything to do with your daughter."

All of the servants agreed to these remarks by nodding their heads.

Emad-Shevets was shocked! He began working his mouth as if to say something, but no words would come out. Finally, he looked a bit sheepish and told the workers to go back to their duties.

"I will have a talk with Hoshi. Let's hope we do not have to have this conversation again." He huffed and turned toward his house, as he called for one of the house servants to summon his daughter.

"Whew!" said Guron. "What has that girl been telling her father? This makes all of us look as if we are ready to molest her."

"That is one of the reasons I don't have anything to do with her," said Jakobi. "Women like that will have you hanged or slaughtered!"

Guron nodded. "Or you will disappear as has happened before, according to the shepherds and the townspeople.

Hoshi is too forward for my taste. The women of my village never walk as she does and would never approach a bunch of men without a chaperone, father or brother walking with her – or at the least have her face veiled!"

Jakobi was not sure of the nationalities of his fellow workers, but there were times when they would mention certain areas outside of Egypt, Arabia or Idumea. He once thought Ranal was Egyptian or Ethiopian because of his dark skin, but during one of their conversations at mealtime, Ranal had mentioned something about having cooked Syrian food for his "master." Was he Syrian, or had he once been a Syrian servant or a slave?

All of the men spoke Aramaic and used their hands for the words of which they were not sure.

He had already learned that it was best to not ask too many questions, for no one had ever questioned where he came from. They only knew he was a Jew because Emad-Shevets always summoned him by loudly instructing the house servants to "go get the Jew." It also informed Jakobi that he was the only Jew who worked for him.

The men silently headed back toward the pig styes as they kept their thoughts to themselves.

24

It seemed the rain would never stop. For three days the water constantly came from the sky. Canaan was known for their famines along with their spasmodic rains, but generally it rained in the early morning and cleared up before noon. Or, if it rained throughout the night, by the time everyone was out of their beds, the sky would be clear or partly cloudy for the rains would have cleared.

The pig styes were nothing but puddles and deep mud. The pigs loved it!

The grunting and snorting from the pens were loud. They enjoyed wallowing and rolled and played the entire time the rains fell. The young piglets were no better than the adults. They tumbled over each other, splashing in the puddles and tripping across the wet ground. A few even got their heads caught in the fences. Many felt if they could get their heads through the fence, the body would follow – not allowing for the fact that their bodies had grown larger than their heads.

The men sat around doing absolutely nothing. They began to talk about their lives before coming to Emad-Shevets' farm. It took some time before Jakobi was able to open up to tell them about his life before arriving in

Canaan. He mentioned how foolhardy he had been to leave his home.

"I have an older brother named Eliakim who tried to tell me what to do with my allowance," he mourned to Etufi. "I was selfish and on my way to becoming a drunk. Eliakim tried to help me settle down, but I felt he was being the bossy older brother and refused to listen to his advice."

Etufi laughed. "I am the older brother and my younger siblings ignored any advice I would give them. Who was I to tell them what to do? We were from the same parents, lived in the same house, ate the same food. They felt there was nothing I could tell them. You should listen to your brother, Jakobi. They have been through many things that you have not yet come up against."

Etufi's smile resembled Eliakim's smile which seemed to be the 'big brother' smile.

Jakobi told the men about meeting his friend, Abijah, and through talking with him began to see how wrong he was in leaving home and family. He believed if he had stayed, perhaps he would now be betrothed or setting up his own home, or even married and having children around.

"I would most definitely have a wife and perhaps servants who could cook decent meals," Renal agreed as Guron nodded his head while laughing. Heber did not say anything but looked contemplative while the others made their comments.

As they waited for nightfall to go to bed, the men could hear the pigs grunting and shifting around in the mud.

Those stupid swine were probably waiting for morning and their next meal.

The next morning, the rain had slowed, but continued to keep the farm muddy. As the men walked toward the eating area, all ate just enough so their stomachs would not growl.

The house servants were told to take the leftover food and give it to the pigs. This allowed the grain supply to be mixed with the human food and spread out over the troughs.

Jakobi looked into the troughs and decided mixing the grain with the gruel made the pigs' food look more appetizing than what was served in the food building. Still, he continued to eat very little at mealtimes.

It had rained before but never consistently for many days. The men knew that their pay would be low the next time — for when it rained they could not work. And if one did not work, one did not get paid.

Even the meals were less appetizing than on sunny days. Perhaps it seemed that way to the pig servants, but they found that all the servants were complaining. The first day, the meal was less than pleasing and by midweek, it was more than horrible. Jakobi could barely stomach the meals that were set out for the workers.

At least the house servants could eat the leftovers from Emad-Shevets table, but even they mumbled about the fare. Yet, their master's family was still eating good food and drinking even better wine. However, it seemed his other servants could not say the same.

* * *

Emad-Shevets stood in front of his house after eating a good meal and watching the rain as it continued to fall. He noticed very little work was being performed and the only ones enjoying the weather were the pigs. His horses and cattle continued to bunch themselves under trees and bushes keeping their heads down, or slowly walking across the pastures to eat the weeds and what little grass they could find.

As he turned to go back into the house, he thought he saw a slight movement toward the back. He walked around back and to the side but did not see anyone.

"Eyes must be playing tricks," he scratched his beard as he mumbled to himself. This is the second or third time he thought he'd seen someone or a shadow or profile. "I must be tired," he thought, and went back into his house.

25

Eliakim leaned against a large olive tree and surveyed his burgeoning olive groves. The many trees had developed tiny blossoms, which let him know that olive fruit would soon appear. The area was beautiful and fragrant for the small, white and feathery flowers were indicative of a full crop. He saw a few of Hannah's servants walking through the groves and knew they, too, were observing the future crops. It takes a few years for the trees to give blossoms, for the tree itself must mature in order to put forth the tiny olives.

He loved looking at his wife's handiwork. Even his father did not have the type of groves he was now observing. His father's groves were beautiful but not as plenteous. After they were married, Eliakim originally planted a few trees to satisfy Hannah, for she loved olives for cooking and pressing for oil. After three years, he had his first harvest. Over the years, she had enlarged his groves. Hannah felt they would save money by cultivating their own olives rather than purchasing olive oil each year.

Hannah had a group of eight personal servants who would soon harvest the many olives and sell them in the marketplace. She allowed one of the small grove areas to be cultivated by them. From this separate section, a small income was made and she allowed those servants to split some of the income from it. She took a small portion of the proceeds and those eight servants divided the larger portion among themselves.

They sold their oil in town and when the people found their olive oil was not as expensive as the foreign traders, their business grew. Many landowners sent their servants to pick up oil from them for cooking and other uses, such as perfumes and pomades. Her servants sold the oil at a common price and made a good profit; everyone was happy. Hannah made sure her shelves were full for the family's use.

Eliakim believed this was the reason his wife's personal servants never quit his household. His shepherds and field workers may find other positions, but not Hannah's. At first he was against her plan, but the growth and sales of the olives kept his wife happy. She had become quite the entrepreneur. His love for his wife made him cautiously agree to it. Few women of whom he was aware had their own businesses; and few servants were paid by the householder as well as gained added income by working their portion of the crops.

Recently his wife told him, "Those who do not work, do not share." There was never a problem with that aspect, for she worked alongside her servants.

Hannah had a good business head and was a great money manager. He tithed, his wife tithed and she made sure those who derived the added income tithed also. All of her servants were not Jewish, but they all complied by donating their income to the synagogue and contributed alms. Her belief in Yahweh caused him to believe that the blessings they received were because Yahweh favored their sacrifices.

The only time she took a break was with the birth of little Ruth, his beautiful baby girl. Although servants were available, she still made sure Ruth was never far from her – carried in a basket, on her hip or tied around her back. His sons loved their little sister and never let her out of their sight when she first began to walk.

Over the last five years, she had pressed the olives they grew for oil and used the remaining orbs as seasoning in food. The first few years, the olive crop was not very large, but with the expansion of the groves, his grain, as well as his herds and sheep, Eliakim and Hannah had become quite wealthy. Even his sons were learning more about handling money and business transactions by watching their parents than what they were being taught in the Hebrew schools.

His sons, Jesse and Obed, were named by his wife because she felt they were names of success. A man is known by his good name, she had told him, and knowing his Jewish history, found this to be true.

He closed his eyes and gave praise to the Lord for giving him a wonderful wife and mother and two intelligent sons. He chuckled to himself for he believed if they had produced another son, his name would have been Boaz. He was grateful for his baby girl.

As he surveyed the land from his area beside the tree, he knew Yahweh had blessed his family. He also wished his younger brother could share in the Lord's many blessings by having his own family and lands. If only he knew where Jakobi had gone. At least he now knew Jakobi was alive, as reported by Abijah.

Slowly he made his way back toward his home. He could see Hannah's slim figure standing in the doorway talking with one of her servants with little Ruth on her hip.

"Ah, Father is right! It is a blessing to come home to a good woman!" he said to himself.

26

The scrambling noises awakened Hoshi. She had not been sound asleep, but lay on top of her bed. Although she had gone to bed a few hours ago, she found sleep would not come. Her father had been very angry with her and barely spoke to her at the evening meal. It wasn't as though she was bothering the servants. She really had no one to talk with, except her mother and a few daughters of the servants who were always occupied. The only ones close to her age were the servants who worked around the pig styes and they had little to do with her and avoided her because of her father's orders.

No, she did not like the pigs. They constantly squealed and smelled horrible, rolling around in the dirt or mud and barely had anything to do with the grass, except nibble the bark around the trees. But the men, Jakobi, Guron, Etufi, Ranal and Heber seemed to always be laughing and enjoying themselves. They told jokes and did not seem to mind that she sometimes followed them. Except today and that was her fault.

Her father berated her and told her that young women never went around men without a chaperone – either her mother or their housekeeper. How could she dare to try to talk to the servants! It was time she knew her place.

Emad-Shevets began to realize it was time to find his daughter a husband. It did not matter that she would have no say-so in the arrangements, but he would make sure she was secure, for although he was stern, he really loved Hoshi. He could have made betrothal agreements with any of the fathers in the area, but was waiting for someone who fulfilled his ideals. It wasn't as if he didn't realize young girls had sexual thoughts just as young men, but she was green and would make a mistake that would embarrass both him and his wife.

Her parents failed to realize that Hoshi was lonely. She was an only child and her father had no female servants close to her age to converse with. Thank God her mother took a lot of time with her. The only time she had other females to visit was when prospective suitors' parents brought their daughters along with them when they called on her parents. She didn't know any of the girls her age on a personal basis and became shy around them. The young men came to look her over as if she was a sow they wished to purchase. She knew her father wanted her to marry well, but most of the young men were only after her father's wealth, not her.

She slipped her feet into soft slipper sandals and tiptoed toward the opening of her room. Her instincts told her to call out to one of the servants or her father, but she knew he was still angry after learning that she had been traveling near the servants by the pig styes.

Once again she heard the soft scrambling and followed the sound. Peeking out of the front of the house she did not see anything due to the darkness, for there was no moon. Must be a servant getting something to eat, she surmised.

Suddenly she was grabbed from the side and a hand closed over her mouth. Her scream came out muffled as her eyes tried to search through the darkness to see who held her captive.

The man started clumsily dragging Hoshi away from the house as she struggled against him. He clutched her tightly by her upper arm and headed toward the shed where the servants fixed grapes for wine or pressed the olives for the kitchen. Her night robe had risen to her thighs and she could feel the cool night air against her skin. She began struggling much harder as she realized what he planned to do with her.

Baring her teeth, she stretched her neck and bit his forearm as hard as she could — tasting the blood that began to pour out of her teeth marks. Frustrated, knowing she drew blood, he slapped her hard across the side of her face and she felt her head wobbling backwards. For a few moments she saw stars as she screamed again.

He then placed one of his hands around her neck, cutting off her air supply and halting her scream. When she began loudly choking, he tried to cover her mouth with the other hand.

Suddenly her assailant quickly released her and she fell to the ground on a sob. She hazily watched as the man seemed to fly backwards against the side of the shed. He tried to scramble to a standing position, but another body was in his way. She watched as one of the servants punched the man in his face. The blow was so loud that she winced.

Within minutes there were four more men beating him; he didn't have a possible chance of protecting himself. Through a haze she recognized her saviors were the men from the pig styes. Etufi, Jakobi, Heber, Guron and Ranal were all throwing punches at the man's body and head. Etufi picked the man's body up by his robe and punched him in the face with a sickening blow.

She looked at her assailant and realized she had never seen him before. Although her throat was sore from the choking, she screamed as loud as she was able. She could hear movement coming from the house and saw her parents and most of the house servants running toward the five fighters.

Her father ran toward her with a large scythe in his hands and her mother was screaming as she ran behind her husband. Emad-Shevets, although a big man, moved quickly, passing up younger servants when he saw his daughter on the ground. Looking to the left, he saw two men in a fist-fight, with four others standing to the side, ready to help if needed, as Etufi punched the man. The other men from the pig styes blocked the man when he tried to get away. The one punching the man was Etufi, but he did not know the other man.

Immediately, the house servants began grabbing his daughter's captor, separating him from Etufi. Although he was winning the battle, Etufi still got in one more punch to the man's face before he, too, was separated by the servants.

"What is going on here? Hoshi, are you all right? Who is this man and where did he come from?" Emad-Shevets was so angry he could hardly speak.

His wife went directly to Hoshi's side and wrapped her arms around her daughter. Both began to sob hysterically.

Emad-Shevets ordered his servants to drag the man into the olive shed and for Etufi and the others to follow behind him.

The man's face had begun to swell and all could see he would have a black eye and facial bruises in a few hours. He was bent over and since the top of his outfit had been ripped off, they could see one of his ribs sticking out. Etufi had a few bruises, but it was very noticeable he was the victor. He was breathing heavily as he began brushing himself free of the dust and mud as he walked behind Emad-Shevets. Although the rain had stopped, the ground was still wet.

Hoshi and her mother followed as they held on to one another as she tried to explain to her mother what had just happened. Emad-Shevets was ready to tell the women to return to the house, but at the look on his wife's face, he decided against it. Only Hoshi could explain what had just happened.

A female servant came forward and wrapped a large blanket around Hoshi, who clutched it as a lifeline. Her mother helped to wrap it more securely around her shoulders since most of the servants were men.

Another servant brought a wet cloth and placed it against Hoshi's head, dabbing at the sides. It was then she noticed that she too was bleeding on the side of her face where the man had slapped her and split the skin.

Quickly, the male servants tied the intruder to one of the poles near the olive barrels and were then dismissed by Emad-Shevets. None of them, however, left the area of the olive shed, waiting to see what would happen next.

27

Hoshi's father laid aside his scythe and went toward the back wall where various tools were hung in order. He reached over and pulled down a snake whip from one of the nails on the wall and wrapped the leather thong around one of his hands. Hoshi and her mother could see the popper or end of the tail was braided tightly and knew the sting would be tremendous to anyone who felt the crack of his whip.

"Tell me, my dear, what happened tonight?" His love for his daughter was tremendous and to almost lose her made him see red.

Etufi stood to the side of the bound man. Hoshi released herself from her mother's side and ran toward him. She touched his bruised hand and holding it between her hands began sobbing as she repeatedly thanked him. Because she was incoherent, no one really knew what she was saying but Etufi looked somewhat embarrassed and gave a slight smile.

Emad-Shevets silently watched her and said nothing. Realizing the pig servant was the hero of this fiasco, he turned his head to stare at Etufi, who rubbed the bloody knuckles on his right hand.

Etufi was not a small man. He was very muscular with long dark hair which was tied with a thin leather strip in a ponytail, and carried himself well. His coloring was tanned from outdoor work and had piercing brown eyes. His soldier-like stance was not missed on Emad-Shevets, who had never really paid much attention to him before. In fact, he had never seriously looked at any of the other men in front of him as he was doing now.

Embarrassed, Etufi kept his head down and pointed his other hand toward his friends, acknowledging their help in subduing the assailant. He was suddenly tongue-tied.

Haltingly he began to explain.

"We were on the way to our barracks when we heard a funny noise. We went to the area beside the house and didn't see anything; although we knew we'd heard some scrambling noises. We noticed nothing was happening in the yard but it was getting dark so we figured it was either a servant moving around or a night animal scrounging for food."

"Then we heard your daughter screaming and ran toward the back of the house. We saw this man dragging your daughter toward the olive shed in back and ran toward him." Etufi pointed to the assailant.

"After I saw him hit your daughter, I caught up with him and hit him. My friends and I kept him from getting away and began to beat him. We were doing so when you came out of the house."

Hoshi nodded in agreement with his explanation. Her tears had dried in dirty running streaks down her face, for she had rubbed her eyes and cheeks with the dirt on her hands from falling to the ground.

"Father, I heard the noise too and came out of my room to see what it was. The next thing I knew, I was grabbed and dragged toward the olive shed. I knew I should have called you, but you were so angry this afternoon, I didn't want to bother you and decided to check it out myself. I'm so very sorry I did not call you."

She began to sob uncontrollably again and went back to stand beside her mother, who wrapped her arms around her daughter and directed her toward the house.

Emad-Shevets dismissed his servants for the night, advising them to get some rest and their duties would resume a bit later in the morning. He then turned toward Etufi and the others and said he would summon them on the morrow.

As all the servants left the olive shed, they heard the sliding sound of the door quietly closing behind them as the captured bleeding man sobbed loudly slumped against the building's middle pole where he was tied.

No one heard another sound during the night.

28

The five men went back to their barracks. No sounds were heard from the olive shed during the night and it was believed that all the servants had returned to their sleeping quarters. As the sun arose in the east, a rooster crowed announcing a new day.

Jakobi wondered if everyone actually fell asleep when they returned to their beds. He went over the actions of the previous evening before falling asleep. He refused to dwell on the captured man and his punishment by Emad-Shevets. Canaanites were not known for being sympathetic and he wondered what happened to the other man that tried to talk to Hoshi prior to his arrival at the pig farm.

Emad-Shevets summoned the five workers to his meeting room following their morning meal. None of the men had ever been inside of his home and began to surreptitiously look around. The room was beautiful in their eyes.

Jakobi thought of his father's meeting room. The curtains that covered the door were not as nice as in his father's room, but close to it. The wooden table was not as large, but he felt Emad-Shevets' room was nicely furnished. A woman's touch was evident as there were flowers and small figurines near the hearth where a small fire was burning.

He smelled a fragrant incense in the room yet was not sure where the scent was coming from, for there was no smoke in the room. Strange, the pig smell was not evident. He did not want to stare at the figurines and thought they may be small Canaanite idols. He knew many non-Jews worshipped various gods, but he had very little knowledge of his master's religious beliefs.

It was no secret to the men that Emad-Shevets was not known to worship in the groves on his property, although many of his servants did. He also knew Canaanites tended to bow to many icons and statues. Although there were Jewish synagogues on the far outskirts of Canaan, he did not know of a place nearby where any type of religious ceremonies might take place.

Emad-Shevets looked directly at Etufi as he moved materials and parchment aside.

"Tell me what you know," he ordered.

Etufi looked straight into the man's face and began.

"For the past few months, I've been noticing someone hanging around the area. Sometimes near the pig styes and other times by the barns. At first I thought it was merely my eyes playing tricks, but the other day I noticed him skulking behind the buildings. I could never get a good look at the man, but the way he was sneaking around, I believed he probably was not a servant. By the time I would reach that area, he was gone. The other day we discussed that we'd all seen someone lurking behind buildings and near the house."

The other men nodded their heads in agreement.

Jakobi stepped forward. "I saw him a few times lately, but the other day I saw him and when he noticed me, he then disappeared. I went after him and later Guron and I both went after him, but he would suddenly disappear. I never saw his face but thought perhaps you had decided to hire more workers and he must have been one of the new ones. The other night we all realized he was trespassing, so we kept a look out for him."

Emad-Shevets looked at the workers and nodded. "I have not hired any more servants, but the other day I thought I saw someone, but just for a quick moment. When I saw him again, I knew it was not my eyes playing tricks. He must have been the same man. I do not have lookouts near the house, but on the outskirts in the event someone was trying to make off with one of my animals. The house servants tend to watch this area."

After staring into the hearth, he turned toward the men and offered his thanks for saving his daughter. He then turned back to study the fire in the hearth.

He advised them that he has taken care of her assailant and that they should return to their duties.

As the men headed back toward the pig styes, the sun began to move from behind the clouds.

"What does it mean," asked Ranal to the others, "that he has 'taken care of the assailant'? I went to the olive shed earlier and there was no sign of the man, no blood or anything – yet there is clean straw on the floor of the shed. I don't know if he changed the straw or had one of the other servants to do it. What happened to the man and what did Emad-Shevets mean?"

"I don't know," answered Jakobi, "and I really don't want to know."

The men silently continued toward the styes.

29

"After last night, you'd think he would be more appreciative and give us better food today! Good food would have been a great reward since we knew we would not be getting more money!"

Etufi looked in the pot as he dipped the gourd inside to get a to get a scoop of the evening meal. "Even the pigs' food looks more appetizing!"

Jakobi also thought the food would be much better this evening. All of the men knew they would not receive more money, but Emad-Shevets could have offered at least one good meal for saving his daughter. Being a Jew, he did not eat pork, but fresh vegetables would have been nice instead of the same gray slop.

That night, Jakobi sat on the side of his bed and picked at the straw that was coming through his blanket. He looked at his clothes and thought about the nightclothes he used to wear. Now he wore the same clothes at night as in the day. His clothes were more ragged than before and he only had two changes of clothing, both ragged. He and the others were still in the same clothing they had on when they arrived at Emad-Shevets' pig farm. The only time their clothes were washed was when it rained and they stood outside near the fences. If the pigs smelled, then so did they.

He remembered the many changes of fine clothing he used to wear. He used to take his clothes and food for granted while living at home. Gupta and the house servants always made sure clean clothes were at his disposal and at mealtimes, he was used to sitting down to a wonderfully prepared meal being brought to him on a platter, not something scooped up from a pot.

His mother and the kitchen servants always sat down together and discussed the meals for the next week, being sure to have on hand enough meat, fruits and vegetables for what they planned. When company arrived unannounced, there was always enough to entertain guests.

His sisters were also included in the decision-making and Salome was already proficient in housekeeping and entertainment skills. Her math skills were much better than his own. He doubted Hoshi knew how to even prepare a meal, entertain unannounced guests, or measure barley. She seemed to always be outside the home, in the yard or walking toward the pig styes. Did she know how to work a loom, sew or darn? Was she aware that food is cooked in pots?

No matter. Emad-Shevets and his wife would make sure Hoshi married a well-to-do suitor who could afford enough servants to do whatever needed to be done in the kitchen.

His mother always made sure her children were dressed nicely. All of his robes were of the finest materials and when one was soiled or torn, another one was available. His parents furnished better clothing for their servants and the food was much better than pig slop. He'd never known the servants to complain – not even the shepherds.

He never knew what Matthan's servants were paid, but knew it had to be more than he was being paid for his hard work with the pigs. When he thought about it, he realized most of his father's older servants were there when he was young and some of their offspring also worked for his father. He did not know what they ate, but it certainly was not pig slop!

Finally, Jakobi came to a decision. It was time to return home.

30

Putting a few items in a small burlap bag, Jakobi said his farewells to his fellow workers. Etufi said he knew it would not be long before Jakobi left. He could see the discontent in his face over the past few months growing worse the longer he stayed. He knew it was not just the lousy food and the poor pay, but he believed Jakobi suffered from homesickness. He was beginning to feel the same.

The five pig workers had been together for some time and had learned quite a bit about each other over the last few years. It was only during the rains that they actually had a chance to talk about their homes and these last three full days of rain gave them a chance to really talk. Their first topic of conversation was always the horrible food and how each missed the food in their villages and towns and in their individual homes – especially fresh fruits and vegetables.

Lately Jakobi had started opening up more and more to the pig workers about his home life, mentioning his parents and his sibling when the rain kept them inside.

He talked about Eliakim and his wife, Hannah, and their two boys. He compared the beauty of Jewish women and how they took great pains to stay clean and smell good;

he could not say the same of Hoshi or her mother. They had been around pigs so long that the smell was in their pores and they did not recognize that they had an odor.

Guron mentioned how surprised he was when they were called to Emad-Shevets' business room.

"I could not believe my nose that the room smelled really clean." All the men agreed.

Being around other pig merchants, Jakobi could understand why Hoshi's suitors had varying odors associated with pigs. Etufi mentioned that he was raised around pigs, but never had a lot to do with them for his father's servants took care of everything associated with them.

He also felt the young females of his village would never have gotten out of bed to check out a noise, especially if there were servants and other adults around.

"Watchmen are always on duty for the protection of the areas against raiders and other perpetrators, and especially within calling distance if there was a dangerous incident. I cannot figure out why Hoshi would decide to check out a mysterious noise. Even if she didn't want to call her father, she could have called upon one of their many house servants."

Jakobi could see Etufi's infatuation of Hoshi was gone.

Ranal, who generally spoke very little, began to discuss information about his culture.

"I don't know if you've ever heard of them, but there are men called "seekers" who go after another area's women, capture them, and take them home to become their wives. I believe that although it is against the laws of many villages and nations, it still occurs. A long time ago, if the man could not find a woman they wanted for a wife from among their own people, they would go into other areas, seek one out and subdue her."

"They have been known to sometimes rape the woman, making her an outcast from her family, causing the father to willingly release her to her rapist because no other man in her village would want her."

Heber nodded his head. "I thought the practice of seekers was outlawed. I do understand it still happens, which is why some of the men of my village strictly protect their women so that such an occurrence does not take place. When my great-grandfather was alive, he told me he became a seeker when there were no women to marry in his village. He decided to go to another area to get the woman he loved. That is how he married my great-grandmother. He sought her out and brought her to our village. Of course she had seen him a few times previously so she came with him willingly and was not raped."

"She eventually fell in love with him and they had many children. You don't hear of that practice any more. Of course if he had not been a seeker for my great-grandmother, I would not be here."

He laughed at his remarks as the others stared at him.

"I believe the man who tried to capture Hoshi was either a seeker or a rapist. He probably saw her somewhere and fell in love with her." Heber closed his eyes in remembrance of a story he was told as a child.

"My father told me about a time long ago when there was a problem about a lack of women during his grandfather time and the men had very few females to marry. This was a time when the tribe of Benjamin did not have enough women, so they were allowed to secretly choose the young virgins in Shiloh who danced during a feast. When the young virgins danced during a celebration, the man would hide, choose the woman of his choice from the Shiloh festival, then grab her and she would become his wife. This allowed the men from the tribe of Benjamin to marry, otherwise the tribe would have died out. I think this may have been when the practice of seeking began."

Jakobi stared at Heber and began to wonder if he was a Jew, for what he said was a part of Jewish history. He vaguely remembered this story from his Jewish history class. ‡

"Where could he have seen her?" Etufi questioned. "She doesn't go anywhere and I've never seen her or her mother leave this farm the entire time I've been here."

"It was a horrible time for the woman. Even if she came to the man willingly, there are those who would still rape her just for the fun of it."

The other men shook their heads.

"My father always made sure my sisters were chaperoned or traveled with servants." Jakobi was confused by this information.

Guron looked at Heber in amazement. "I have never, ever heard of this practice."

---

† *See Book of Judges, Chapter 21*

Etufi gave a slight smile. "If Hoshi had been raped, Emad-Shevets would have tried to keep it a secret. He knows it is time for Hoshi to be betrothed by now, but he's still taking his time. All the suitors we've seen coming to his house are very well to do. They would not want a woman who has been raped so her father's dreams of making a financial alliance for his daughter would have fallen through. And if she is made pregnant by the man, she might meet an untimely death."

"If that man was a seeker and is in the hands of Emad-Shevets, he will never live to see another day. That is, if he is still alive, which I sincerely doubt!"

Etufi closed his eyes and went into deep thought.

"You know, it makes me realize that my village has a lot of beautiful women who are clean and always smelled nice. I guess it took yesterday's happenings for me to realize that my village is really where I need to choose my wife. The woman I choose needs to be a person who would make a wonderful wife and mother and not one who flaunts herself in front of other men."

All of them shook their heads, looked at each other and began to head toward the styes.

* * *

For the first time in months, Jakobi ate a heavy morning meal, knowing he did not want to travel on an empty stomach. It still tasted horrible, but he knew he had to prepare for his trip home. Taking a few victuals from the food room, he went to the servants' barracks.

He went to Emad-Shevets and received his final pay. Emad-Shevets invited him into his business room and gave his resignation. He had the impression the man was expecting him for it did not take him long to count out the money and place it in a small drawstring purse. When he later checked the purse, Jakobi saw that he was given a small bit extra. Perhaps Emad-Shevets gave the extra pay for helping in the capture of Hoshi's assailant for he did not believe it was a mistake on his employer's part. He gave his thanks but there was no handshake or pleasantries given. Jakobi left the house and went to see his fellow workers.

After saying his goodbyes to his friends, Jakobi gave a great hug to his friend, Etufi, who said he would be leaving soon himself. He set out that morning with a small bag of stale barley bread, raisins, and weak wine in a goat-skinned bag and headed away from the pig farm toward home.

"Home," he thought to himself. "A place where there were no pigs in sight or slop on the table. Sometimes it takes a change of circumstance to appreciate what you once had."

31

It seemed to Jakobi it was taking longer to go home than it did to leave home. As he plodded on, he thought back to the day he left home. His mind wandered toward his mother and her tears as she hugged him. He could still feel her face against his chest. She had laid her head there and softly patted his face. The last thing she said through her tears was, "Be well, my son, be well. Yahweh will always be with you."

Had Yahweh been with him when he made his decision to leave? Did Yahweh keep his presence near even though he had worked with unclean animals? He had not had a decent bath in so long that he wondered if the smell of pigs rose up to the Lord instead of a sweet smell. Had Yahweh been near although he had sinned against Him?

Whenever he bedded down for the night under the stars, each shining light had the faces of his family. One night he fell to his knees and asked Yahweh for words to say when he reached home. After walking for many days, Yahweh had not answered his request.

Passing through deserted areas, he saw vultures and a few mountain lions. He never slept in the open, but in a place where the animals would not bother him for he had seen the remains of wild animals that had been prey to other animals. After hearing howls and screeches from animals he could not identify, he had picked up a large stick and began using it for walking as well as for protection. No animals came near him as he trudged on, but he was always wary of the wildlife in the places he traveled.

He once came to a small river and had to figure out how to cross it. He remembered paying for a ferry when he crossed it the first time. He knew the ferry fee was not the amount he should have been charged, but since he had worn fancy clothes and had his animals, he knew the charge was quite high. This time he had no extra funds for the fare; he decided to find a low section to the river that he might be able to cross.

As he started across, he felt it was at low tide for the water was indeed low, but halfway across the river it suddenly came to his knees, then his hips and finally above his head. Thankfully Eliakim had taught him how to swim. His meager belongings were immediately soaked, along with the last of his barley bread and figs. Slowly he turned over on his back, letting his now wet bag sit on his stomach as he back-stroked to the other side. Reaching land, he stood on the muddy bank and watched the last of the sun as it sank below the horizon.

Thank the Good Lord the warm air quickly dried his clothes and body. Jakobi's arms ached from the exercise and he was so tired he began to silently cry as he began to set aside his items so they would dry. The bread was soggy and falling apart, but he chewed on his figs slowly, trying to make them last a long time.

He thought of his sisters, Salome and Rachel. They, too, had cried — especially Rachel. No matter his behavior, his youngest sister never thought ill of him. He was, after all, her big brother. Eliakim was an adult when she was born, so she was closer to him than to her older brother. She was so overwrought she could only hesitantly say softly through her tears five little words: "I'll always love you, Jakobi!"

Salome never said anything, but her eyes told him she loved him and would miss him. Now that he thought back, he remembered the two girls hugging him, but did he hug them in return? Crying as he passed through small towns, he continued onward.

My, how his heart hurt!

He never saw his elder brother or his father. Matthan always made sure his children felt his love whenever he had to travel on business. He once told a friend to be blessed when he entered the house, and when he left, Matthan said the same. As family and friends left the household, they too were told to "be blessed" as they walked out the door.

When Rachel asked why he said those words, father had replied to her that people should be blessed when they arrive and blessed when they leave; for scripture says we should ask the Lord's blessings on those who come in and those who leave out.

Father never said a word to him prior to his leaving. What were his thoughts? He knew Father had been hurt by his request to get his inheritance; yet, he never said, "no." Legally, he did not have to give him his inheritance because he was still alive. He could not know his father's thoughts when he requested money instead of cattle and sheep.

Falling to his knees, Jakobi yelled into the air, "I'm so sorry Father. Please forgive me!" Still remorseful, he again screamed, "Yahweh, please forgive me. Allow me to do what is right in Your sight."

The birds around him began screaming from the noise and flying from their nests in the trees from his disturbance.

Eliakim had either gone back home to his family or was in his fields and he never had the chance to know how his brother felt about his decision to leave home. He really missed his brother.

Many times Eliakim had tried to help him make decisions about his future and he never listened. His brother had told him many times, "Jakobi, you never listen!"

Eliakim was so right.

Jakobi knew Eliakim's feelings were in turmoil about his decision, but he felt Father would still have a son around. It wasn't as if Eliakim had to be around to do chores or watch over the animals. Lord knows, Father had enough servants to do what needed to be done around the household and on his properties. He should have gone to find Eliakim before he left home. Although his brother knew of his discontent, he still should have confided in him before leaving.

So sad, he thought, so sad! Too late smart!

Abijah had told him his family mourned his leaving. Did they mourn because they thought him dead, or because of the way he left?

He never tried to make contact with his family during the entire time he had been gone. If he had not spoken to Abijah when he went to get the grain, he would not have had any news of his family. Abijah promised to take his message to his family. What if Abijah did not give his message to his family, especially to his mother and sisters? He hoped his words were delivered.

Thinking of Abijah made him consider what he lost. Abijah had said his sister used to have a crush on him. Zyama had wanted him to begin thinking of married life and the only girl he really had any feelings for was Abijah's sister, Ramani. Even if he was rich and Ramani showed interest, Abijah and his father were the doorway through which he would have to enter. Although Ramani's father was a good friend to Matthan, he was aware his younger son's former lifestyle left a lot to the imagination.

And even if her family allowed him to court, he had nothing to offer her. He was aware that she had been around the men in her family long enough to help make investment decisions similar to Hannah. He remembered that Abijah used her housekeeping knowledge to make his home more comfortable. Wise women were hard to find.

He now understood the help Hannah was to his brother and what his mother was to his father. It takes a wise and good woman to stand alongside her husband, to help a man expand in his business dealings, and help him consider vital decisions. It also took a good and loving woman to manage a household and give him the reassurance a man needs to make the household comfortable.

Many men did not consider a woman wise, but he had learned over the years, it's not always the pretty face or form that a man must consider, but also her mind. If not, what would you talk about over the breakfast table? He knew he did not want giggling all day for his wife. The pretty face was an added asset and Ramani had it all!

32

Jakobi slept in areas he was sure his mother would be appalled to know. One night he stopped to rest in a small oasis and found a brush area when he heard camels and people coming toward him. Travelers or a small caravan, he guessed as he scrambled to pick up his belongings and hide behind a small strand of trees and bushes. Not sure if the people were friend or foe, and hopefully not bandits, he thought as he quietly settled where he would not be seen. It just now occurred to him that there might be bandits during his travels.

On his trip before, he never ran into any other travelers, except once. He had followed a group of Levites for some time; knowing there was safety in numbers. Of course, he didn't have to travel on foot that time, nor did he have to bed down in the open areas, for he, his horse and mules had stayed overnight in comfortable inns – that was when he had money to do so.

Toward evening a few of the men wandered near his hiding place to urinate, so he made sure he was well hidden. Hardly breathing, Jakobi kept as quiet as he possibly could, moving further into the brush area in the event others would also venture toward him. He was glad he had a few pieces of bread and cheese left to appease his hunger; and was very happy he had filled his water skin from the small watering hole earlier.

When the travelers left the next morning, he stayed near the oasis for one more night and then began his trek once again. It was his plan to give the travelers time to move on before he ventured forth.

* * *

On another night, as he passed outside a near-deserted village, he noticed small caves in the hillside. Passing a few of them, he decided to take lodging in one he felt was unoccupied. He climbed up a small hillside and found a small cave he thought would be a great place to sleep.

Just as he entered, he could smell rotting flesh and knew it was the cave of a leper. As his eyes adjusted to the darkness, he found a small, thin body in a fetal position. Covering his nose, he knew it was the body of a middle-aged leprous man who had recently died.

He stood over the body for a few moments, noticing the many boils on his body. Many of his fingers and toes were stubs where some of his digits must have rotted and fallen off. Jakobi had seen lepers before on the outskirts of his hometown, but never up close. He started to step out and go look for another place to bed down, but he began to feel compassion for the dead man.

His father would sometimes send a servant with food bags to be left on the edge of town to feed the lepers that lived in the hills near the synagogue. He had never paid much attention to this, but if food was not placed somewhere near them, many would die of hunger.

When he asked why he was sending food to the lepers, Father told him, "The lepers are the 'ignored ones.' They cannot go into the cities to beg alms, for no one would come near them. And should they receive any alms at all, who would sell them food? Thus," he said, "it was up to those who have – to feed those who have not."

His thoughts conflicted. It was bad enough that the man was leprous, but he died with no family or friends standing around. To be eaten by animals and not having a decent burial began to worry him. Poor man.

Was he Jewish or Gentile? Not noticing any religious tattoos, he concluded the leper may have been Jewish for the Gentiles were noted for having tattoos which showed the deity they worshipped. Did he have family? Had he been living for a long time in this small cave? Did anyone even know he had been living here? Jakobi could feel tears welling in his eyes and turned away from the sight.

Finding a large flat stone, he went outside the cave toward a small sandy area nearby. He took the stone and slowly began digging through the soft dirt to a depth of more than three feet. It was hard work, but he thought of his family's area on his parents' land. There was a section on the property where members of his family were buried or entombed, and another area for servants who had passed away.

If he had died while he was away from family and friends, he would be in the very same circumstance. No one should die alone, he reasoned; and without someone to see to their remains. It was heartbreaking. He had a dog once that died and remembered that he and Salome had made sure its small body had a resting place. His sister even said a small prayer over the grave.

After a few hours, when he gauged the grave might be deep enough, he began to collect medium and large rocks he found nearby. By the time the sun began to rise, he had found a tattered blanket in the rear of the cave and, holding his breath from the stench, rolled the body into it. Pulling the blanket, he was able to semi-wrap the body without actually touching it, pulled it from the cave and slid it into the hole. Little by little, he took his hands and threw handsful of dirt on top. Methodically he placed stones on top of the makeshift grave. At least the animals would not smell it or bother the grave.

If he was home, he would be considered "unclean" for having been close to a leprous body; however, he figured he hadn't been to a religious service in such a long time that he was not going to worry about it. Breathing heavily from exertion of pulling the body into the grave, he felt some words should be said over the man, but did not know what words to say.

"I'm not a priest or even a Levite," he whispered, "but you deserve some comforting words."

He looked up to the sky and began to quote a scripture he barely remembered. He wasn't sure if he could quote it correctly, but felt it was the best he could do. Although he was not of the priestly tribe, he felt it would be remiss if the man happened to be a Jew to not say something.

'Here goes, my good man," he whispered. He prostrated himself on the ground and said something he felt could be used as a prayer:

"We are nothing but dust and will go back to the dust. So may Yahweh watch over the two of us, please Lord, while we're absent, one from another. Selah. (sigh) That should do it!"

He made a quick decision to make sure he attended synagogue when he returned home. He had almost forgotten some of the scriptures and prayers he had been taught. He thought back to his father saying something similar to his impromptu prayer when people left his home. Shaking the loose dirt from his hands, he stood, stretched, and sent a thankful prayer to Yahweh for the fact that he was alive and had family to return to.

His muscles and brain were telling him he was tired, but thought it wise to not venture back into the cave. Wild or scavenging animals might still be able to smell the remains of the rotted body and go into the cave to explore.

He did not want to be caught inside sleeping, so he picked up his meager belongings and his traveling stick and moved on. He walked until the sun began to set once again.

33

Jakobi was hungry for he had eaten the last of his food, and so tired he was ready to drop. Going into a small town, he found a stable behind a small inn and stealthily climbed a rickety ladder into the hayloft. He slept through most of the day and awoke when his stomach began to growl.

Quietly flexing his muscles, he heard people below him transacting business and realized the stable housed horses and mules for people in the city. Although it was still light outside, it was too late to travel, so once the voices stopped, he quietly stole down the ladder and went into the small village. There he found a few foreign vendors and purchased dates, goat cheese, dried fish, a few pieces of barley bread and a skin of weak wine. That night he proceeded to wolf down the food. After the meals he had been eating, the food was like a banquet.

After appeasing his hunger, Jakobi went back to the stable and climbed once again to the loft, sleeping until the sun began to rise. On his way out of town, he purchased a few more food items, packed his few things and started the day's travel.

* * *

Jakobi continued to travel and smiled as the areas began to look familiar. There was the small watering hole in which he used to swim, and he was very happy to see sheep and cattle. The green grass was very even from the sheep and camels having eaten the blades. The herds were being watched by shepherds and other servants, some of whom he immediately recognized.

His heart lifted as he smiled for he knew he was now on his father's property.

Immediately, he stopped.

Sure he was almost home, but what would he say to his family? Would his father even recognize him? He had lost a lot of weight and his long, untrimmed hair and scraggly beard made him appear unkempt. Even his clothes were ragged. He knew his mother would blanch at the way he now looked. She always kept clean robes and decent sandals in his wardrobe area. He had not worn sandals in so long a time that he wondered how his feet would feel in sandals. The servants in his family's household wore sandals and decent clothing.

Would he be welcome? He was no longer the second son of his father for he had given up that right as well as any other privileges.

Mentally he began to rehearse his speech to his father as he continued walking. He would ask to be a servant in his father's employ and knew it would be a privilege after being in the employ of Emad-Shevets. And, even better, he would sleep in a decent bed and not have to eat pig slop.

He began to pray to Yahweh as he had never prayed before. He asked the Lord to allow him to find favor with his father, and prayed his family would not hate him for leaving or for returning.

34

One of the younger shepherds sighted a man coming over the rise. Running up the hill, he pointed the man out to his father who would know if the man was friend or foe. His father grabbed a club and started to tell his son to tell the other shepherds to be on the alert. He stopped mid-sentence as he tried to see if he could identify the man, for his stride was familiar. Cupping his hands above his eyes, he squinted into the sun to see if he could identify the traveler. The older man began to smile.

"I believe – yes, it is – it is Jakobi!" His excitement carried over to his son and was contagious. "Hurry my son! Hurry and let Gupta know Jakobi is home!"

Running to the homestead, the boy found Gupta training a new servant in one of the back rooms. Breathing heavily, he imparted the news to Gupta saying his father recognized the man. Gupta, in turn, sought Matthan who was in the room where he conducted business.

As Gupta quietly knocked on the wooden beam leading into the room, Matthan looked up.

"I have news, my lord. Your son has been sighted coming through the south pasture."

Matthan stood up and started to walk toward the hearth. "Have Eliakim come in and bring him here. He has probably come to discuss an investment he and I are arranging."

"No, my lord, not Eliakim," was the quiet reply.

Matthan looked up and his eyes held hope. "Are you sure, Gupta? It has been so long!"

"Yes, my lord. The shepherds have informed me that it is your son, Jakobi, and he is on his way here."

He reached out and put both hands on Gupta's shoulders and squeezed twice.

"Thank you, Gupta! Thank you!"

Matthan stepped away from the desk and Gupta could see that in his excitement he was a bit unsteady on his feet. Quickly regaining his balance and composure, Matthan hurried to the front of the house.

At that moment, Zyama came from one of the back rooms carrying a few bowls.

"Matthan, dear, so many of our bowls have cracks, I have decided to order new ones and I know how you hate to make decisions about such mundane matters, but I'd like you to look at these bowls for when we entertain."

Noticing no reply, she looked up at her husband, showing concern. "Are you all right, Matthan? Is something the matter? Are you ill?"

She quickly hurried toward her husband.

"He's come home, Zyama. He's come home," he whispered.

As realization dawned, Zyama sat slowly into the nearest chair.

"Jakobi? Jakobi is home?" Her eyes were very wide with surprise, and then they began to shine with tears.

Matthan patted her shoulders and hurried through the doorway.

Reaching the nearest part of the south pasture, Matthan knew without a doubt it was the form of his son walking toward him. "Praise Yahweh," he breathed.

As Jakobi realized it was his father, he began to walk faster. Then, throwing aside his walking stick, he greatly increased his stride into a run. Gupta stood beside him for a few seconds and placed his right hand on his master's left shoulder. Matthan smiled at him, girded his robe and ran toward his son who also began to run toward his father.

As they met together, both began babbling at the same time. They grabbed at each other and hugged tightly, crying as they did so.

"Father, I have surely sinned against you and the family, as well as against Yahweh. I am truly sorry. I'm not worthy to be called your son. Please forgive me for the hurt I've given you." Jakobi tried to speak hurriedly to make sure he spoke all the words he wanted his father to hear. He knew without a doubt that he was babbling.

"Jakobi, it is so good to hold you once again. You will always be my son for you are the fruit of my loins. Yahweh has blessed me to see you alive and well."

"Father, I have sinned against heaven and shamed you and the family. I have worked with swine after misusing my

inheritance. I am no longer worthy to be called your son.
I beg of you to make me like one of your hired servants!"

Gupta came alongside Matthan along with two other
servants. Matthan turned toward them and quickly gave
instructions.

"Quick, Gupta! Have a servant prepare a bath for my
son and after he's washed, bring the best robe and put it
on him. Bring new sandals for his feet, for no son of mine
should be barefoot." Gupta nodded to one of the servants,
who ran toward the house.

Whispering so that only Gupta could hear, he
instructed him to check the family chest and look for a
small pouch which held the family ring which belonged
to Jakobi.

"Go, find the ring and put the family ring on Jakobi's
finger."

"You," he pointed his finger toward the other servant,
"have the kitchen staff prepare a fatted calf and roast it.
We shall celebrate the return of my son, for this son of
mine was thought to be dead and yet lives. He was lost
and is now found!" Matthan was jubilant.

Within a couple of hours, Jakobi was back in the fold
of most of his family. His mother had wrapped her arms
around him as if he was a hurt child and kissed his head,
cheeks, and chin. His sisters wrapped their arms around
him tightly. The servants were also happy and even they
were allowed to stop their chores in order to join the
celebration. Matthan had provisions prepared not only
for his family and friends, but for his servants as well.

35

Eliakim left the north pasture as he headed toward his family home. He could hear music and laughter way before he reached the area. He saw one of the house servants heading toward the house from the rear and asked if there was a party taking place in his parents' home.

"Yes, my lord. We are celebrating the return of your brother. Jakobi has come home and your father has asked that we prepare the fatted calf, for we are celebrating his safe return. Your relatives and some of his friends are here, including Abijah, his brother and his family. I believe other friends and relatives of your family are on their way.

Eliakim did not say anything, but nodded his head and walked away.

As everyone was laughing, eating and drinking the fine wine that Matthan had the servants prepare for the party, Gupta quickly scanned the room and noticed the elder son was not in attendance. He went to one of the servers and asked if he or anyone else knew where Eliakim might be. It was very noticeable the eldest son was not there.

One of the servers replied to him, "I saw him heading toward the stables. He may still be there."

He saw Jakobi speaking with Abijah with his arms around Rachel's shoulders. He was smiling as people came up to welcome him home. Once again Jakobi was dressed in a fine robe and had beautiful leather sandals on his feet. Although he was thinner than before, and his skin was a golden tan from working outdoors, he still looked to be in good health.

* * *

Gupta went in search of Eliakim and found him in a grassy area behind the stables. The older man watched him for a few moments. Eliakim sat on the fence rubbing one of the donkey's heads. His shoulders were slumped as one of his hands scratched behind the ears of the animal.

Finally Gupta headed toward the house and sought out Matthan, who stood to the side watching the celebration of his family, friends and servants. All types of food and delicacies were being served by the servants as well as vessels of fine wine from his vineyard. It was reminiscent of the bar mitzvahs that had been held when the boys were younger.

"My lord, your elder son is outside the stables and refuses to come to the celebration," he whispered. "You might want to ask him to come in."

Gupta bowed and left to give further instructions to the servants who were supplying the food from the kitchen.

Matthan had informed Gupta to tell the servants to rotate their services so that each may also join in the celebration. He was exultant!

Matthan nodded his head and slipped away from his guests. He found his elder son sitting quietly on the fence. The music in the background was almost raucus. He turned toward the house and watched as servants scampered to and fro from their service areas toward the celebration.

Father clapped one of his hands on his son's shoulders when he reached him.

"Come, Eliakim, join in the celebration for the return of your brother and greet our guests. It would be well for you to attend as the host of a party given for his brother."

"Host?! Father, I am surprised at you! Your son, my brother, left us for years. We had no word from him as to whether he was alive or dead. He took his share of his inheritance as if you had already died, and now he returns — and I'm supposed to celebrate?!! I didn't throw this party! What? Celebrate that he used his inheritance to spend time at wild parties with harlots and unsavory men and then go to a heathen country to have a good time? He left our home a rich man and I'm quite sure he returned with nothing!"

His face was flushed as he stared at his father. "Yet, look at you, the host who has left his party to entreat me to attend!"

Eliakim was so angry his eyes began to blur as he continued his rant.

"I have never asked anything of you — not money, not honor, nothing! All these years I have worked your property as well as my own. I have never disobeyed you and have done whatever you asked. Yet, you have never killed the fatted calf or even a skinny goat for me so that I could celebrate with my friends! The spoiled stripling decides to return home and now your favor for him seems to fall into place!" His words ended on a sob.

Matthan could see the anger and sorrow in his son's eyes and he felt his hurt. Wrapping his arms around him, he also began to cry.

"My son, it has always been my hope that you knew that I love you. You are my firstborn and the gem of my loins. Whether you stayed or left, I would always love you. Everything I own will be yours as an inheritance, not only as the firstborn, but as a beloved son. But your brother who was dead is now alive. He was lost, but is now found."

"You see, he also, is a part of me. Please come with me to the celebration."

Matthan held his hand out to his elder son, and waited knowing Eliakim was weighing in his mind his decision. He could only hope that Eliakim understood his reasoning for giving the party and the love he felt for both of his sons.

36

With Eliakim walking silently beside him, Matthan was still very sad. He knew his elder son's agreement to attend the party was only out of duty. His decision had nothing to do with love for his brother, but love for his father.

As the two men headed toward the house, Matthan turned to Eliakim.

"I pray you'll at least look pleased as we enter. I would hate for friends and family to see you looking so sad."

"Father, you know I am always pleased to enter your home."

* * *

Eliakim greeted the many guests and with his mother's prodding went to stand beside Jakobi. Jakobi gave a tentative smile and the two men greeted guests together, but finally walked toward the back section of the house where they could be alone. Eventually, they walked around the back garden.

"I know you hate me," Jakobi started. "I did not mean to hurt our parents or sisters, but especially you. You should know I did not come back to try to get any part of Father's inheritance, since I have already used mine. But to let you all know that I missed you."

"I don't hate you, Jakobi. Sure, I supposed you missed us, but never thought to send back word to the family that you were alive or even where you had decided to settle. Mother cried for days and our sisters walked around with sad faces. Father keeps his feelings to himself, but I could see he was hurt also. I was hurt, but more so for our family. You've always been somewhat spoiled and I accepted that. But when you requested your inheritance, I really wanted to choke you when I looked at Father's face."

Jakobi put his head down but did not respond to his brother's statements, for he knew what he said was true.

"I don't know if I can even make it up to everyone, but I will try. I hope to meet with you in a few days. I would like to explain some things and tell you what I had been doing while I was gone. My life away was not a great experience, but I want you to understand what made me come back home."

"That's not necessary. You've returned and the family is happy once more. That is what counts." Eliakim continued walking.

"The family is happy, but what about you? I know there is anger in your face, but I want the entire family to forgive me. Can you forgive me, Eliakim?" Jakobi stared at his elder brother.

Eliakim eventually stopped and looked at his brother for some time. "You seem somewhat muscular, but I also see you've lost weight," was his only reply.

Eventually, he began a conversation to bring Jakobi up to date on his family, ignoring his question.

37

"No, no, no! I will not have my son eating with the servants! Do you hear me, Matthan? I will go along with most of your ideas, but never that!" Zyama was adamant, waving her hands and did everything but stamp her foot.

Her husband knew there would be some disagreement to his plan but he never thought his wife would become so angry. He looked at her in surprise. She never went against any plan he suggested in connection with the outdoor servants. She was a dutiful and obedient wife who felt as ruler of his house, whatever he said she always agreed. But not this time!

She was so angry, she was shaking. In all the time they had been married, Zyama had never shown this much anger. He looked at her in amazement.

His wife was an older version of Rachel. Long brown hair, covered in a beautiful scarf with a matching robe. She was impeccable in dress, speech and action. Her skin was as smooth as when he first met her. He had always loved her as a youth, but at the time of their betrothal, was not sure she loved him.

Matthan knew she had many suitors and he was one of many, but decided to have his father offer for her. When

Zyama's father consulted with his daughter, happily she said yes. He was very surprised that she was asked by her family, since many betrothal agreements are made without consulting the female.

He told himself that if he ever had any female children, he would make sure they were aware of any proposals before he would agree to make a contract. He need not have worried, for he knew Zyama would take care of that matter, which she is doing with Salome.

Zyama was still pacing and ranting as he brought his mind back to the matter at hand.

"We're talking about our son, Matthan, our son! He can dress like a servant, even work like one in the fields, if you will, but I am putting my foot down when it comes to leaving him out of taking his meals with us. He is my son as well! He is family!"

"If HE so chooses to eat elsewhere, then I could see. But to ban him from the family table is wrong! I want him to always be welcome at our table!"

"I don't care if he and Eliakim are estranged; he will not be such at our family table!"

Zyama turned her back to her husband and stormed out of the room. Matthan chuckled as he started to go after her, but decided to let her cool off for a spell. He had already decided he would go along with her wishes.

"My lord, she's a real spitfire today!"

38

Eliakim worked hard with his sons as the three helped in the delivery of the small second lamb. Obed looked serious as he helped his father and brother try to hold the ewe's kicking legs. The mother was squirming as she tried to help in the little one's birth. Her bleating was loud and agonized.

"The other came out much easier, Father, but this one seems to have had a problem. It didn't even try to help itself."

Jesse held the newly born lamb and shook his head. "I don't know if this one will make it, Obed. She's so little and does not seem to have any energy. The other one showed more energy, but this one seems to be somewhat limp although its breathing is not labored."

Obed looked as if he would cry. "What shall we do, Father? I hope it doesn't die. The ewe has turned her head and doesn't even want to nurse her. She accepted the first one, but not this one. If she chooses not to feed her, she will surely die."

Keeping his hands on the ewe, Eliakim shook his head. "We didn't know the mother was having twins, son, so I'm quite sure that she didn't either."

"We'll see what happens after we wash this one off and then put her next to the mother again beside her brother. If she feeds the little one, we'll know what to do next; if not, we'll have to make other plans for her. Perhaps we'll see if one of the other ewes will allow this one to nurse." Eliakim watched his youngest son who now held the little lamb, turning slightly to lock eyes with Jesse, who shook his head.

"If none will feed her, may I have her father?" asked a teary-eyed Obed. "I'll nurse her myself. If she doesn't make it, then at least I tried. It has got to be hard on the little one to make her way in the world. Someone has to help her. If not, she'll die."

He put his head down and lovingly smoothed back the small animal's wet fur as he whispered, "Don't worry little one, we'll find a way to keep you alive."

Jesse and Eliakim looked at each other and quietly shook their heads. There did not seem to be much hope for the newborn, but neither had the heart to inform Obed.

* * *

Hannah stood in the doorway of the small shed where her husband and sons were still kneeling on the hay-strewn floor. She could see two new lambs, one much smaller than the other, one was bleating more loudly than the other.

"Ah," she thought. "All that work for a small runt."

She knew the small lamb did not have a possible chance of survival. She started to enter the shed, but for some reason hesitated and backed out of their view.

Obed had his head down as he held the smaller one, while Eliakim and Jesse were clearing the birth area, putting down fresh straw. None of the three had noticed her standing there.

"Of course, son. Let's see what happens over the next day or so. I don't want you to keep your hopes up, but we'll see. Yahweh has created animals to try to survive. It is only humans that take it upon themselves to give up and die. Yet sometimes when animals look as if they can't make it, they are known to sometimes rebound and try to live. This little one may be one of those animals."

"Sort of like Uncle Jakobi, hunh Father? He tried to die, but rebounded and is now back home. Grandfather said he was dead, but is now alive. Yahweh created him to live, so he decided to do just that! Right, Father?"

Eliakim did not say anything to his remark, but continued moving the straw around on the shed's floor.

At that moment, Eliakim looked up and noticed his wife standing there. As their eyes locked, Hannah did not say a word, but nodded her head and quietly turned around, heading back toward the house.

As she walked away, she smiled to herself.

39

A few months later, Eliakim went to the property that was now Jakobi's new home. The sheep he had been given by Eliakim and Matthan had begun to recognize him whenever he went near them.

There was one small lamb that tended to turn to the left when the others turned right, but Obed was there with his small crook to grab him back.

Obed had received permission to raise his small lamb on his uncle's land and came daily to observe his lamb's growth. Everyone, including Jakobi, thought the lamb would not see one or two weeks of life, but the little furry ball was romping with other lambs — the smallest and the most energetic. His father had given him a small wagon and young donkey in which to ride directly to Jakobi's property once his home chores were finished.

One of the younger shepherds fashioned a small staff with a crook with which to watch the lamb and instructed him on what to do whenever it strayed. It amused Matthan's shepherds to see him so conscientious concerning the welfare of his runt. Obed took it upon himself to begin watching all the lambs, which gave the younger shepherds the opportunity to pay more attention to the larger ones.

Very seldom did they have problems with lions or other predators attacking the sheep, but they always kept a watchful eye just in case. They also kept an eye on Obed, making sure Matthan's grandson did not get into any trouble. When they saw how diligent he had become, it was easy to see that the lad could take care of himself.

As Eliakim's large horse came over the rise, he hailed his brother. Behind him came another horse with a new halter. The second horse was not as large, but was a beautiful brown color and looked similar to Eliakim's. When Jakobi came near, they hugged and headed toward a small grove of trees to which they tethered both horses.

"Your small farm is doing well, I see. In just a short time period, you've got this property looking very prosperous. I came to offer you this horse," he said as he patted the second horse's nose.

Jakobi went toward the horse as he felt its forelocks. "He's beautiful, Eliakim. Thank you so much. I've been using my mules to get around the property. My next purchase would have been for a good horse, but not as good as this one."

"Well, my brother, this is payment for allowing Obed's silly little lamb to live on your property."

"Come now, that lamb cannot be eating that much grass and I really do not have to do anything for her. Obed takes good care of her, as well as a few other lambs that have been born since I took over the property."

"Well, the horse is a small investment and should help as Father tells me you are extending your land and herds."

"I want to thank you, Eliakim. I know you didn't want me to know, but Mother told me you purchased this land for me, as well as gave me the starter herds of sheep and cattle. After all that's happened, you're still trying to help me. I do plan to listen to you from now on. Perhaps in a few years my crops and herds will be able to show better income. I hope this does not subtract from your inheritance."

"Just so you know, Jakobi, the inheritance means nothing for I am almost as wealthy as Father. Yahweh has added his blessings to the growth of what I have. Since you've been gone, my herds and crops have more than tripled. My sons are doing very well, as you could see at your party; and Jesse, the eldest, has purchased a bit of land with his allowance. He is now betrothed to one of our friend's daughters and I believe it is a love match. Of course, they will not marry for some time, but he has already increased his small holdings. His herds are growing and he will possibly be able to support a wife and family in a few years."

"Obed is doing very well in school and is trying to learn as much as he can from me concerning sheep and cattle. My sweet daughter, Ruth, is in good health. In looks and mannerism, she takes after Hannah. Not only is Ruth beautiful, but she has an intelligent mind. You've already met her for she was born since you've been gone."

"Obed has been teaching Ruth some of the things he's learning in school and we are finding that she catches on very quickly to be so young."

"Hannah's olive crop was large last year and seems to be even larger this year. She and her servants have purchased a new press for oil. They used to do it by physical means. We've been blessed. Our crops were not touched by the disease of the caterpillar. Her servant kept a close watch because olive trees only bear fruit after a few years. It takes so long for them to blossom for they don't do so the first couple of years."

"When Hannah disappears for a few hours or so, I know she's with her servants in the press room."

"Press room?"

"I had to add on to the olive shed because it gets dark early and I don't like them working in the dark. It has windows and faces the house. She has named the area the 'olive press room' and now she's got me saying that. Sometimes I forget and still call it the shed."

Jakobi came to a halt, causing Eliakim to hesitate. He faced his brother and looked at him. The two men stared at each other for a short time, then Jakobi grabbed his brother, put his arms around him and began to cry.

Eliakim was taken aback. He held himself stiffly at first and finally wrapped his arms around his younger brother, patting him on his back. Eventually he, too, began to cry.

"I am so sorry for what I did to you, Eliakim. I did not mean to hurt you. While I was away, I always heard your voice in my head repeating, 'Jakobi, you never listen. Jakobi, you never listen.' You were so right! I did not listen, and I have only myself to blame."

"I had asked Father to make me a servant in the household, but he and Mother refused. I know I will not inherit and have no problem with it, but the main thing I want is for us to be friends. Not just brothers, Eliakim, but friends."

"While I was away, I began to realize many things about myself. I even spoke with Abijah and found that unlike me, he listened to his father and brother. He is doing quite well, you know."

Eliakim nodded his head. "Yes, I know. I've watched him mature. He has a large spread on the other side of his father's land and owns many herds of sheep, cattle, and even fig and olive groves. Hannah has been giving Abijah tips for his groves and told him it might take a few years for his olive trees to mature before producing a nice harvest."

"I believe he wants to offer for Salome, but Father and I have been letting him cool his heels for awhile. With his new responsibilities, he seems to have matured."

"Truth to tell, Salome does not seem adverse to his attention, for he is well-liked and seems to know his own mind. We realize she would be well treated by Abijah because he seems to care for her, and his family loves her. They would make a good match. I must say, he looks at our sister with love in his eyes." He chuckled at this remark.

"I recently learned from Gupta that one of the servants acted as chaperone when she was with Rachel, Salome and Mother in Abijah's mother's house for an afternoon brunch. Rachel knows a lot of the servants' families there and was able to play games with their children."

"However, it seems Salome and Abijah were able to privately converse with the chaperone in the background and without the mothers constantly watching them. This, you know, was a ploy by the parents to see if it would be a good match. The two mothers set this up and we may be celebrating a betrothal in the very near future."

"Personally, I believe it was the plan of both mothers to see how Salome receives Abijah's attentions. I guess they're now satisfied. Mother and Nihomi are very close and this will allow them to become even closer."

Eliakim and Jakobi stopped for a moment to watch a small herd of sheep grazing beside a large tree. They smiled at one another as the lambs dance around their mothers; and once again the two men continued walking.

"I went by your small house or your 'hovel' as you call it. Very nice. Father told me he has been paying you wages and I see you've got a small family of servants."

"Yes, Father has been generous. I know his servants do not make as much as he's paying me, and although he says its not an allowance, he's still being very generous."

"As for my new servants, believe it or not, they came to me. Banna's husband recently passed away, but she has three helpful sons who are hard workers. Although they are different ages, I still get them mixed up."

"Ezra helps me with the sheep and cattle, and I believe he loves that type of work. Abni has started a small house garden, for he likes working with the soil. I was able to purchase a team of oxen and together he and I sowed the land and planted grain and other seeds."

"The third son, Simon, is proficient in wine making, for it seems he was taught by his father, as well as being an accomplished smithy. He told me he was apprenticed to a master blacksmith as a youth, but the master died. He was unable to attach himself to another master smithy so he did not complete his apprenticeship. He's very good, Eliakim, for he has forged new tools for me that is as good as a master's work."

"I told them from the start that I cannot pay them a lot, but they don't seem to care right now because their father was the breadwinner and he's gone so they had no place to stay and there is no income. As my income increases, I'll soon be able to increase their wages and, hopefully, they'll stay with me. They're all honest and hard-working."

"They didn't say and I didn't ask, but believe they were servants in a large estate. First, their father passed away, then their former house burned to the ground under shaky circumstances. When their father passed away, their master did not require the rest of the family. When I told them I could use all of them but I had no place for them to stay, they told me not to worry; they needed positions. The family had been staying with cousins in a small home and it was time they moved to a place of their own."

"Within a week of working for me, they began constructing a house for themselves on the property. Their cousins and friends came to help and in no time at all, they have a comfortable place on the other side of the ridge. They've also moved the few personal belongings they salvaged from the fire into it; and with their first pay purchased household goods. They've even fixed up my small house and added a larger room in the rear. You'll have to see what they've done."

"Someone in town told Banna they believed I was in need of servants, so now I have a cook, an extra shepherd, a farm master, and a handyman."

"The woman is a wonderful cook and as you can see," he patted his stomach, "I am enjoying decent meals. I still take some of my evening meals with the family, but I've informed Mother that I would not always be at the table. She understands and father is happy I'm showing some independence."

"I am enjoying my new home. When I fall into my bed every night, I am very tired, but there is a feeling of satisfaction. Father understands, but mother still wants me to take my Sabbath meals after going to the synagogue with the family. Banna and her family are Jewish, so they celebrate the Sabbaths and the high holy days along with me. That's good because I was the only Jew on the pig farm and did not celebrate the sabbath days."

"I now understand how you felt when you were starting up your property and household."

Eliakim smiled at the pride and joy in his brother's voice.

"I have noticed you've been attending services at the synagogue and it seems like old times for the entire family to be in attendance. Your nephews are so pleased to be sitting with you. Obed loves you, Jakobi. You were always his hero, and more so since you took in his lamb. He tells me you gave him more lambs to oversee. It seems he has been taking his responsibilities in earnest."

"Believe it or not, Eliakim, I really did not attend services in Canaan, because I didn't believe I needed Yahweh. My excuse was that there was no synagogue around, but I could have found one if I really wanted to go. I had my own agenda; then when I started working at the pig farm, there was no time."

"I really enjoy them now, and sitting with your sons is great! They help me remember the words to songs I've forgotten. You know, it's funny how you stay away from the synagogue for a long while and forget the psalms. But later, you try your best to remember scriptures and songs that can help you realize who Yahweh is and how His presence has not departed from you. Life is more than religion and Yahweh is more than the God we take for granted."

Jakobi looked like he wanted to cry as he said, "I am humbled, Eliakim, I am truly humbled."

He grabbed Eliakim's arm. "I still want an answer to my question, Eliakim." Jakobi looked his brother in his face. "You never answered my question from when I first came home."

Eliakim looked confused. He put his head to the side trying to remember his brother's question.

"And what question is that?" he finally asked.

"Can you ever forgive me for what I've done? Although we get along pretty well now, I know we can never be as close as we used to be prior to my leaving, but can you honestly forgive me?"

Putting his hand on Jakobi's shoulder, Eliakim answered, "Yes, Jakobi, I do forgive you. I prayed to Yahweh to not harden my heart against you. I'll admit it was hard to forgive you in the beginning, but I have. We will always be brothers and I hope brothers who will always love each other. Yes, I forgive you."

40

That evening Eliakim walked to the rear of his house to sit with Hannah as she and her servants worked with her new olive press. He kissed her cheek as he greeted the group. She and her servants did not miss a beat while pressing the olives for the oil.

"Ah, my husband. You came to see the olive crop being pressed. This machine is wonderful and saves us a lot of time."

The servants with her smiled and nodded in agreement.

"Jesse told me you were riding over to see your brother. Is he well? How are his new servants working out?"

"Oh, yes. He's doing just fine. And those servants you recommended are doing fine, too. They've even put up a place to live on the property. I don't think they needed any references — either that or Jakobi didn't ask it of them. He was just happy to have help.

"I am so pleased. When I asked Gupta if he knew of a family of servants in need of positions, he was happy to tell me of Banna and her young sons. Since her husband passed away, they've really been struggling because they had no other income. Then to add to their misery, their small home caught fire and burned to the ground; but blessed be, they had relatives who could take them in for a spell."

"They didn't want to intrude on their small space, so they were almost desperate for work. Some of your father's servants told Gupta about their plight and he interviewed them before sending them to Jakobi."

"Gupta told Banna if they were asked how they knew Jakobi needed servants, they were to only tell him that someone in town suggested they see if he needed help. By the time Gupta saw Banna again, she reported they had been hired by your brother and she owes everything to him. Now everyone is happy."

"Well my dear, let's just pray that it does not come up that you and Gupta were behind their hiring."

He thought for a moment. "You know, at this point, I really don't believe it will cause a problem."

"By the way, I just want you to know Jakobi told me that Mother has told him I purchased the property for him. She did not tell him I purchased it with the money you and she gave me. You women keep a lot of secrets. I know you make extra money from your olives, but I also believe Mother has been skimming the household funds Father gives her."

Lifting one of his eyebrows, Eliakim looked at his wife, who put her head down, seemingly concentrating on the many olives rolling into the wood and stone machine. She did not make a response to his silent inquiry.

"I'm not going to ask how you both were able to save so much money and then have it available for a sizeable land purchase."

Standing up, he put his hands on her shoulders and gave her a quick squeeze as he quietly said, "Good night, my dear. You need to get some rest for tomorrow is another day."

She did not lift her head, but under her loose hair, Eliakim was very sure that Hannah was smiling one of her secretive smiles.

41

"I can't believe your father said 'yes', Jakobi. I almost fainted. If I was a little girl – or a pig, haha – I would have squealed!" Abijah was exuberant.

"Not only will be I be your best friend, I'll also be your brother-in-law. Yahweh is so good!!"

The two friends stood on the side of Matthan's business room with celebration wine in hand, surrounded by relatives and friends from both families.

Salome's smile was from cheek to cheek as she was being hugged and congratulated as much as Abijah. The betrothal agreement had been written and agreed upon and everyone had gathered together to celebrate.

"I'll tell you, Abijah, if I ever find out you are mistreating my sister, you'll have me, Eliakim, his sons and little daughter all over you!"

"No problem there, Jakobi. I love her and believe she loves me. I was sweating so much that I had to look down to make sure there was no puddle on your floor. I had wanted to ask for Salome's hand before, but I was afraid of your father's answer. I had discussed this with Salome at another friend's betrothal and knew she would say 'yes.' Yet I could never find the right time or the nerve to ask your parents. My mother is just as happy. She loves Salome and is very happy about my choice."

"I had approached your father a few times," he admitted, "and even tried to throw some hints to Eliakim, but both of them would either change the subject or, before I could get the words out, they would seem to walk away from me. I guess I was taking too long to get my request together. I believe they knew, but were not giving me enough time to get the words out. Whew! I'm glad that part is over."

"Salome will be well taken care of, Jakobi, I give you my solemn promise. You can be sure of that. Although she comes with a dowry, she could be as poor as a servant's sandal and I would still ask for her hand in marriage. I am doing very well for myself, even as a second son and any children we have will be well provided for." Both young men nodded.

"I believe you will, Abijah. After visiting your property and your home, I know Salome will not want for anything."

They went toward a smaller area and Jakobi quietly put his head close to Abijah.

"I also want to express my thanks to you, Abijah, for not telling my family my true situation when you saw me. Eliakim told me that you gave them limited information on my whereabouts and how I was doing. I told Eliakim my entire situation a few months back, but my father has not requested any information, so I've spoken with him in bits and pieces. He and Mother are just happy I'm home."

"I wouldn't worry about it, Jakobi. Just keep doing what you've been doing since you came home and all will be well. Just remember, I will always be your friend."

* * *

Salome and Ramani had sauntered outside to the garden area and were sitting side by side on a small wooden bench. Rachel and her cousins were chatting and giggling audibly in the adjoining small garden. Servants moved among the guests and over to them with trays of cheese, grapes and other fruits, and various breads. Both of them helped themselves to the fare.

"I'm so happy you're going to be a part of my family, Salome. And to answer your question, yes, I will be happy to be one of your bridesmaids. How very wonderful!"

Ramani clapped her hands and hugged her new sister-in-law to be. "I've been watching your brother, Salome, but he doesn't seem to notice me at all. I've always liked Jakobi, even when we were younger. I always thought he was different from my brother's other friends. Some of them would party and drink until they fell over, but not your brother. He drank, but not to excess. Now that he has his own land and animals, he hardly says anything to me, except after synagogue."

"When services are over, he makes a point of walking beside me as my family heads toward home. Although we don't say very much to each other, I have to admit it is a companionable silence."

Shaking her head, Salome grabbed her friend's hand. "I believe he likes you, too, but since he came home last year, he's been more subdued. Father says he's in the process of becoming more mature. Plus, he's been working hard on his property and his animals and they seem to be his main concern right now."

"When he set up the little house on his property, I gave him some hints to make it more livable, and brought over some items to keep his house from looking so stark. When I sewed the curtains and brought them over, his servants helped me to hang them and it changed the entire living space. His housekeeper, Banna, even supplied pottery, eating utensils, oils for burning and candles. I hadn't even thought of those little necessities."

"Believe it or not, his house is looking very smart. When I first saw it, I thought 'uugghh'! But now I really like it."

Ramani put her finger to her cheek. "Perhaps I can suggest to Abijah to visit Jakobi and allow me to tag along with him. I have been creating new pottery and my father purchased a new kiln for burning. I don't want to be too forward, but Abijah might take me if I have a good excuse. He and Jakobi are very close and I think he knows I like his friend very much even though we haven't talked about it. I'll make special plates, bowls and cups for his cooking area."

As she looked around, Salome said, "We'd best go back inside. I see more people have arrived to the celebration and I am one of the guests of honor. I'm so happy we had this time to talk. We'll do it more often between now and the wedding for we have to make a lot of plans!"

The two girls put their arms around each other's waists and continued toward the doorway as many of the guests turned to smile at their entrance.

42

The priests were lined up inside the arches of the synagogue as Abijah and Salome stepped forward through the chuppah or canopy. After the seven wedding blessings were given and the ring placed on Abijah's finger, the wrapped chalice was then laid on the floor by Jakobi for his friend.

The couple held hands as Abijah held his foot high. It seemed as if he practically jumped as his sandal landed on the wrapped chalice. All the wedding guests heard it breaking. Immediately everyone yelled, 'Mazel Tov' and 'L'chaim' ** and began clapping and cheering as the couple kissed.

The Rabbi gave a final short prayer and intoned quietly, "As this chalice shatters, so may your marriage never break as you remember and understand the frailty of life. You are no longer two but one in the sight of Yahweh!"

Another priest followed with, "May your marriage last longer than it would take to put the many pieces back together again."

**Mazel Tov! Congratulations!
L'chaim! To a Long Life!

Obed smiled and clapped along with the family and other guests. He leaned over and whispered to Eliakim, "Father, once the chalice is broken, they'll never be able to put it back together again."

"I know son. It means, the marriage will last a very, very long time, and the couple will never separate."

"Oh!" He gave thought to the tradition. "But Father, what happens if he brings his foot down and the chalice doesn't break?"

"Well, the groom will just keep on doing it until it does!" Eliakim chuckled along with some of the men in the section behind him.

* * *

The guests left the synagogue and headed toward Matthan's home for the celebration. The wedding couple would be arriving shortly as Matthan and Amos, Abijah's father, followed by the brothers, Eliakim and Joash, arrived to give orders to the household servants for the reception of guests.

Servants were waiting at all of the doors as Gupta and his sons directed the guests to seats for the feet washing. More servants were bustling about with trays and pots laden with various kosher delicacies, as well as wine. A complete dinner would be served later in the day for the guests. There were musicians playing in the main hall and adults and children began to enjoy the celebration.

Jakobi waited at the door for Ramani to arrive with her mother. As the family entered the house, Jakobi went to her side. She made a lovely bridesmaid, was gorgeous in a gold veil and dress with a diaphanous silk overlay. All the maids looked very pretty, but he believed Ramani was the loveliest. He could feel his heart racing as he approached her.

Nihomi and Zyama were behind them as they entered the house. Both women looked at each other and smiled. Neither said a word, but from his position at the door, Gupta could not help but notice the look that passed between them.

43

It was with a heavy heart that Jakobi headed for the sheep fold on his property. Over the two years, he was doing much better financially than he had thought possible. He had added more land to his property, as well as more herds. With the counseling and help of Eliakim and Abijah, Jakobi had begun investing his funds, selling some of his animals to other landowners and purchased additional property. He was soon able to pay his servants higher wages and had hired a few additional servants.

Banna was now the head housekeeper over two other women and he and Abni had planted more grain. It was almost time for the harvest and to allow day workers to come on the property to help separate the wheat from the chaff. After discussing with Abijah that the gleaners could be a blessing to him, he remembered his Jewish history about Boaz.

Boaz allowed his future wife, Ruth, to glean on his property and later married her. He was well aware that Ramani would not have to glean and felt the story was one of the romantic ones. But it wasn't Ruth that he wanted; it was Ramani.

For some reason or another, he was always tongue-tied whenever he was around her. They did not talk much but she was comforting to him and they would walk in companionable silence. Whenever they walked together from synagogue or visiting with his sister and brother-in-law, he always made a point of staying around their house in order to see if Ramani would walk through the room, for most times she was in attendance. They would sometimes get an opportunity to talk quietly in Abijah and Salome's garden area with a chaperone present.

The day before, on an errand for his mother, he had gone to visit Abijah's mother and there, in the sitting room, were two young suitors and their families visiting with Amos, Nihomi and Ramani. He had begun to think of Ramani as his, but also knew other suitors were courting her. He remembered his mother and Abijah's mother giving Salome and Abijah time to visit with each other when they realized a match of their children might be possible.

The suitors who were present were young men with whom he once attended parties at Abijah's house. What if they were in the process of asking Ramani's parents for permission to court or, heaven forbid, for her hand?

Perhaps he should talk to his brother before he missed his opportunity with Ramani to another suitor.

* * *

"What is it you're asking of me, Jakobi? Are you telling me you have found a betrothal prospect? I certainly hope so. I've been telling you for the longest that you are in need of a good wife. Who is she?"

Eliakim tried to keep a straight face, for the entire family knew of his infatuation with Ramani. He was beginning to worry about Jakobi's lack of courage in asking for the girl.

"It's Ramani, Abijah's sister. I can't get her out of my mind and I want to ask for her hand, but I can't get up the nerve. After all I've been through, you'd think I would be much bolder. Help me, Eliakim! How did you approach Father to ask him to request a betrothal agreement in asking for Hannah? Did he and mother set up a visit to her parents or did they just happen to be visiting already? Do I go to her or her parents or what?"

"Well, Little Brother, how about first finding out if Ramani wants you. She's a pretty girl and from what I hear, she's had several offers and has turned them down. Her parents have agreed to let her decide the issue. It might do you well to have Father put your bid in now. At least that's what I did."

He had a far-away look as he reminisced. "Hannah had many suitors. Some were her family's connections, but mostly because she's beauiful and has a fine mind. Ramani has a fine mind also."

"Yes, and she's also very beautiful." Jakobi added.

"You should talk this over with Father. I'm advising you to first speak with Ramani. You don't know if she'll have you. You really need to see if she has already made a commitment to someone else. I know for certain she has had some good prospects who have offered for her."

"Goodness! I hadn't thought of that." Jakobi slapped his hand to the side of his face. "I don't have as much to offer as some of her other suitors. She may opt for a man with more money and property. I know that some of the men I used to sow my oats with (as Father used to say) when I was younger are also courting her. A woman and her family have to look at various aspects for her future security. Will the prospective husband be able to keep her in the same fashion to which she has become accustomed; if and when children are born to them, will they be able to afford a family, big or small? If she's a shopper, would she be able to receive an allowance or money for extra household use? Oh, my lord! That's a lot to think about!"

"Well, do you think you can fulfill a future wife's needs as you've just stated?"

"I can now, thanks to Abijah's and your advice! If I had listened to you when I was younger, I would not have to question myself about it now. Please, Eliakim, talk to Father for me."

"Nope, Little Brother. You ask him."

Jakobi's eyes widened. "What? You wouldn't help me?"

"Yes, but there are some things a man has to do for himself. First, go and talk to Ramani and put forth your plea. See if she's amenable to you. She may not mind that you're not as rich as King Solomon!"

"Funny, Eliakim, very, very funny!"

44

"Mother, is something wrong? Gupta sent a messenger to tell me you needed me right away. He seemed to think it might be urgent because it seems you must have fallen. I'm sorry it took so long, but I was in my fields and it took him a while to find me. I hurried as fast as I could."

"Jakobi, I was on my way to visit Nihomi and bumped my knee into the furniture. I'm fine, but would you be so kind as to drive the small dray for me to Nihomi's house? We will be going shopping together and my knee is very sore. I was going to cancel, but we planned this day far in advance. I wanted to use Jesse but he's working on a project for Hannah and Obed is still in school. I would appreciate it if we could go soon."

Zyama was almost afraid Jakobi would not be able to respond right away to her morning message. She and Nihomi had everything in place for the day. Gupta had promised he would fix the message so it would be considered an emergency, so his ploy must have worked. It was less than two hours ago the message was sent.

"Sure, Mother. Shouldn't you be consulting with a physician instead of going on a shopping trip? You can always go to the market. We can send one of the servants, if you like."

"I know, but the rains stopped our previous plans, so today is a good day for shopping. Besides, if you take me in the dray, we will not have to carry any packages and we can be home before the sun sets."

Jakobi went to his father's barns and had one of the grooms hitch the small dray that Salome and Rachel and their friends used. The seats held four people comfortably — two in front and two in the rear. Instead of putting the small, slow mule in front, the servant hitched an older horse in front.

Jumping into the wagon, he clicked to the horse and pulled to the front of the house. Zyama came to the front along with Elizabeth, the servant she generally used as a chaperone for her daughters, also came out the door. Jakobi and the servant sat up front, which left Zyama to sit in the back. It did not take long for them to reach Abijah's family home.

When they arrived, Nihomi and Ramani came out of the door.

"Zyama, it seems Ramani would like to look at new sandals, so she has decided to come along. I hope this doesn't stop us from shopping," Nihomi said, looking sideways at Jakobi.

Ramani looked confused for a second, but quietly walked toward the small wagon.

"Of course not. Elizabeth," Zyama directed the servant, "why don't you have a nice visit with Nihomi's servants. We won't be long. When Jakobi and I return to drop Nihomi and Ramani off, you can get back into the wagon for us to go home. Have a nice visit and we'll see you soon."

Jumping from the wagon, Jakobi helped the servant down from the front seat. Elizabeth nodded, smiled at Zyama and quickly headed toward the servants' quarters in the rear. Jakobi helped Nihomi to seat herself next to Zyama and then held his hand out to Ramani to be seated next to him. Ramani gave a shy smile as she put her soft hands in Jakobi's as he helped her into the front seat. He felt a tingle in his hand and wondered if she also felt it.

The two ladies in the rear began talking to each other in earnest as if they had not seen each other in months, when in reality they visited often and had attended synagogue just the other day. Seating himself next to the young lady, Jakobi turned the dray toward town, driving slowly.

"Where to first, Mother? How about we see where the traders have settled and then you can all get out and walk around a bit. I will keep myself available so any purchases you make can be stored in the wagon. That is, if it is all right with the three of you?"

Nihomi smiled as she said, "That's a wonderful idea, Jakobi. Let's look at the sandals for Ramani first. Then we can go to the section where they sell curtain material. I've been trying to decide what I want to do with Abijah's old rooms. After he moved to his first house, every once in awhile he would stay over in his old bedroom. When he moved into his own home, it has hardly been used. When he married, some of our relatives stayed over in his quarters throughout the wedding celebration."

"Now that he is married, I may fix it as a guest room. You never know who may decide to visit your home and stay over for a few nights."

Zyama agreed. "You know I haven't done anything with Salome's area either. I was going to move Rachel into that section, but she wants to remain in her own room. Fixing it up as a guest area is a great idea!"

"Jakobi, let's change direction, and go first to where the material vendors are located. We might be there for awhile. And Ramani, don't worry. We'll get to the sandal place right after that."

At this remark, Ramani gave a small start, but slowly nodded in agreement.

Nihomi and Zyama continued chatting about how they were going to fix up their added room space as the little wagon moved forward.

45

The wagon pulled in front of a trader's cart that sold a conglomeration of pottery, bracelets, rings and other jewelry, various materials, scarves, etc.

The two women hopped out of the dray without his help; Jakobi watched his mother walk quickly toward the trader's cart, leaving Ramani and himself alone. Although she had her veil across her face, Ramani realized she was left alone with a man and no chaperone. Jakobi looked at her and she stared in return, her eyes as wide as saucers.

"Jakobi, we have been left alone and Elizabeth is back at my house." Ramani was starting to worry about appearances. Whenever she went to the market, it was either chaperoned by her mother, brothers or a servant.

"I know," he responded. "We won't walk around together, but will remain in the wagon. We don't want to cause undue attention to ourselves. This way, we'll look like a brother and sister waiting for someone. Is that all right with you?"

She nodded her head and he was able to see the veil twitch as she smiled at him. Ramani looked around the area and noticed the hustle and bustle of traders, vendors, and customers, mostly women. A few men walked by idly fingering the bracelets as if searching for gifts.

Noticing a cart with scarves, Jakobi thought back to Emad-Shevets sending him to retrieve a load of grain in town. It brought to mind the young girls who fingered the scarves which made him miss his sisters. He shook his head to ignore the pain it had caused.

He looked at the items on the cart. Fluttering in the breeze was a very pretty filmy scarf that he thought would look very nice on Ramani. He wondered if she wanted to make a purchase.

"If you'd like to look at the scarves over there or purchase something, I believe it would be fine to look at the merchandise over on that cart. I've never seen those traders before but their merchandise looks first quality."

He was finding it hard to interrupt the silence between them, but Ramani's veil twitched once again as she shook her head. He tried to think of a safe topic of conversation, but could not come up with any ideas.

In desperation, he decided to talk about his farm. As soon as he began speaking, he thought it would be best to cut it short.

"Two of my ewes had their lambs a few weeks ago and they are growing by leaps and bounds. Obed's lamb is growing and is very energetic, but he keeps a calm eye on all the lambs. My crops are doing very well, too."

After a blank stare at him, Ramani suddenly began to laugh. Not just a chuckle, but a beautiful laugh that made him laugh as well. Soon, they were both almost bent over.

"I am so sorry, Jakobi. There was such a lull between us that I was trying to think of something to say. Then I realized when you started telling me about your lambs that you were doing the same. We've known each other since childhood, so we should be able to carry on a nice conversation. Please forgive me. I did not mean to laugh about your lambs; it's just that …," she gave a small hiccup, laughed, and tried again. "Please forgive me."

"Whew! I was trying to carry on a conversation in which you'd be interested and that's all my mind could come up with. Let's start over again and talk in a civil manner about things that might interest us both."

"Don't worry, Jakobi. I did find your lambs interesting. I'm happy to hear about their births. I had heard about Obed's runt, so its good to know she's still alive. Abijah says you are doing quite well for yourself and you've added more property. What used to be a small area, has now grown quite large. I'm happy to hear of your progress and the fact that you've returned. I did miss seeing you."

Happiness began to seep into his heart.

As she continued, he noticed she had a habit of twisting the end of her veil.

"I used to see you when I visited your brother's house and I've noticed how lovely you've become. Eliakim tells me you're planning on a betrothal soon. So – er, um – by the way, has your family made a decision on which man to settle a betrothal agreement?"

"Father has allowed me to consider the three men who have asked for me. He told me to consider carefully the merits of each one. Two of them you already know from attending some of Abijah's parties. But no, I have not made a decision as yet. He feels I should make a decision soon because I'm getting older and, as he calls it, 'will be sitting on a shelf.'"

It's now or never, he thought. Jakobi offered a short prayer as he tried to make sure his words would be accepted.

"Ramani, I'd like you to consider me as a suitor also – may I be the fourth? I know we haven't been in each other's presence for some time, but I think we would do well together. I probably don't have as much to offer as some of your other suitors, but I am doing very well with my property and my animals. My income has increased and my investments are doing very well. Although my home is small, it is just a starter. Eventually I would like to construct a larger, roomier home with a larger kitchen and more bedrooms. I would also like to visit with you soon – in the presence of your parents or a chaperone, of course."

He turned his head toward the traders' carts, as he awaited her reply. He stopped breathing for awhile as his heart began to beat rapidly. He did not notice the flush of her cheeks as he waited for her answer. Please, please, oh Lord, please! Jakobi mentally implored.

Ramani touched his shoulder, causing him to turn toward her. Her eyes were very large and shining. Although he could not see through the veil, he knew she was giving him a big smile as she nodded her head.

"Jakobi, I would love to have you for a suitor. You are always invited to come visit me – in the presence of a chaperone, of course." Her veil twitched as she gave him another shy smile and looked very pleased.

"I will speak with Father, but I know it will not be a problem. Please do. I will await your visit."

The couple could see their mothers as they went from table to cart, fingering materials, lifting pottery to the sun to peer into bowls, and moving from place to place.

Jakobi noted his mother no longer limped and, thinking back, remembered he did not have to help her step down from the dray. Although Elizabeth climbed into the wagon as a chaperone, there was no reason for her to come along. He did not know in advance that Ramani was coming along to shop and, he believed, neither did she.

It seemed there was no problem for Mother to leave Elizabeth at Nihomi's house since Ramani would be in the presence of her mother. He then remembered that Elizabeth had a relative who was a servant in Nihomi's household.

Slowly it dawned on him that both mothers must have planned this trip for him and Ramani to be left alone in each other's company for a short while. When he looked at Ramani, he could see she, too, understood the reason for them being left alone together in the wagon.

Suddenly he laughed and eventually Ramani laughed along with him. Both of them turned to where they could still see their mothers and noticed the two women were hiding behind the trader's cart observing them in return.

"Oh my, Jakobi! I think our mothers made sure we'd be left alone to get to know each other. Although it was wicked of them to do so, I want you to know that I am very pleased they did for I have enjoyed our conversation."

She reached over and lightly patted his hand. Soon they began a pleasant conversation concerning the weather, then recounted their childhood memories along with Abijah and Salome's wedding.

Jakobi noticed that their conversation was no longer stilted and enjoyed being with Ramani. He made up his mind right then that he would talk to Father today about asking Ramani's father to allow him to be a suitor and, hopefully, for her hand in betrothal.

He did not want to be fourth in line — he wanted to be first!

46

After depositing both Ramani and Nihomi to their house, he drove toward the back of the property to pick up Elizabeth. The chaperone was happy to have had a chance to visit with her cousin and gave Zyama a conspiratorial wink, which Jakobi did not miss.

Zyama and Elizabeth chatted all the way home as if they were long-lost friends. He knew this was to keep him from asking a bunch of questions, but he did not care. He had a lot to think about and wanted to meet with his father right away.

It was his wish to word his request in such a way that Matthan would readily agree. He did not want to flounder for words as Abijah had done in front of his father when he was trying to ask for Salome. Abijah was not a stammerer, but Amos, Joash, Eliakim and his father had a hearty laugh about it when discussing how they both kept putting him off, making him forget what he wanted to say to them. He was a man grown and wanted to be mature about the matter.

He found his father that evening looking over the land behind his home. The sun was just setting and Matthan's mouth was moving but no words were coming out. He raised his hands to the sky and smiled. It took Jakobi a few seconds to realize that his father was praying and giving thanks to Yahweh. He knew his father was a religious man and was known to disappear for hours at a time, even when he was little. His mother always told them that their father would be back soon, for she gave him distance when he went to pray.

He remembered from his childhood that this was his father's quiet time with Yahweh. He hated to interrupt him so he began to turn around and go back to the house, but his father stopped him.

"Is there something you wanted, my son?" Matthan quietly asked.

"I'm sorry, Father; I did not want to interrupt you."

"Come and walk with me, Jakobi. Let's go back to the house where we can talk." Matthan put his arm across his son's shoulders and the two men headed toward the room where he transacted business.

"Father, I have a request and I hope this is the right time to ask it."

Matthan sat behind his desk while Jakobi decided to stand.

"I know you've been wondering when I would take a wife, and I had said I did not see any woman I wanted to marry. But I have, Father, and now I'd like to ask for her hand. I need you to speak for me so that I may set up a betrothal agreement."

"Hmmm," his father stroked his beard in thought. "Have you talked with this young lady and does she feel the same as you, or is this a spur of the moment thing?"

"Oh, no, Father. She is agreeable for me to be considered as one of her suitors, but I don't want to be a suitor. I wish to marry her."

"I see. And who is she?"

"She's Ramani, the daughter of your friend, Amos, and sister of Abijah and Joash. I was able to spend time with her as well as converse with her today and I find she is not adverse to me. In fact, I believe she also has feelings for me. I would like to put forth my suit now because she has other men asking for her hand. I'm praying that my suit will be accepted. She's beautiful and has the kind of personality that would make me a wonderful wife. I explained to her my financial situation and she was not worried about that, although her other suitors have more money."

"I want to be as happy as Eliakim and Hannah and you and Mother. I know that with Ramani as my wife, I will be, but I need to settle a betrothal agreement soon or I may lose her to another suitor. Would you speak for me, Father?"

"When do you want to do this?"

"Right now, if I could, but as soon as possible."

Matthan looked out the window above his son's head and smiled. Ah hah, he thought, Zyama and Nihomi havedone it again. Our families will be forever linked by our children.

"I'll call for one of the servants to take a message to Amos. Let me see if he can set aside some time to see the two of us. I'll send a message tonight and perhaps we'll receive a reply in the next day or so."

"Father, Eliakim is aware of this and I am sure he would be in agreement to go with us — if it is allowed."

"I will send a message to Amos and Nihomi right away. I'm quite sure we'll have a response in no time. Eliakim is expected first thing in the morning and I will notify him of your request."

* * *

"You called for me father? Elizabeth said you wanted to see me."

Ramani walked into her father's business room. He was seated at the table at which he conducted his business dealings and her mother was standing behind him with her hands on his shoulders.

"Yes, my dear. I have in my hands a missive from Matthan. It seems his son, Jakobi, wants to be one of your suitors. He also wants to be considered more than that — he wants to discuss a marriage agreement for you to become his betrothed. I guess he knows you've had other offers and is trying to get his request in right now. I need to get an answer to him right away, if that is fine with you. He, his father and brother will await my reply."

He glanced down at the message and then looked back up at his daughter. Ramani had the sweetest look on her face as he continued.

"I'm leaving the matter up to you, my dear. You know that most women never get that privilege, but your mother and I want to see you happy. How should I reply?"

As she looked at her father's quivering beard, Ramani could see he was trying not to show humor. Her mother, on the other hand, was smiling broadly.

"I need to know how you feel about it, as well as you, Mother, for he would be your son-in-law. As for me, I would like to consider him as my betrothed, Father. I think we shall fare nicely together and I believe he loves me very much. He has told me of his finances and given me information about his property.

"He does not have as much to offer as some of my other suitors, but I feel we will do well together. My answer is yes, Father."

Nihomi came around the room and hugged her daughter. She held Ramani back by the shoulders as she smiled at her with tears in her eyes.

"Do you think you could love him," she asked, "since you say you believe he loves you? As your father said, we want you to be happy. My father allowed me to make the decision about my betrothal, and of my many suitors, I chose Amos. I loved him then and I love him now and we've been happy ever since. This is something we want for you also."

"Oh, yes, Mother. I do love him and always have, even when I was younger. I'm just happy that he feels the same."

Her father glanced at the note in his hand. "I guess I'll write a positive reply. You'll be betrothed soon, but the wedding will take place later for it will have to be planned. Now it is getting late, so get ready for bed, my dear, and we'll talk again in the morning."

As Ramani left the room, she heard her mother exclaim, "Oh, Amos! I'm so happy for those two young people. Zyama and I knew they were in love. Now we have a new daughter and will soon have a new son-in-law."

"Yes, my love, and so will Matthan and Zyama!"

Giving a quiet giggle, Ramani did a little jig as she walked toward her bedroom.

47

Abijah and Joash kissed Ramani on each side of her face in front of their guests. Then all three with Eliakim, Salome and Rachel did the same to Jakobi.

Although the chalice had been broken during the ceremony, everyone was still shouting 'Mazol Tov' and 'l'chaim' while clinking their wine cups. Music was being played as wine and food were being served and eaten in abundance.

When Abijah and Jakobi finally had a moment together, Abijah gave the same warning he received from his friend at his own wedding.

"Okay Jakobi, if I ever find out you are mistreating my sister, you'll have me and Joash and every relative at this reception all over you!"

"No problem, my friend! I love her as much as you love Salome." Both men looked over at their wife and sister as the two women returned the look. All four smiled at each other.

Salome now had a small baby bump as she would be giving birth in three or four months with Abijah's first child. Ramani had her hand on the bump, hoping to feel movement.

**Mazel Tov!*   *Congratulations!*
L'chaim!   *To a Long Life!*

Nihomi and Zyama were in the circle of their friends chattering happily.

Obed and Jesse stood near the buffet table selecting from the fare. Touching his brother's arm, Obed had started talking with his mouth full of food.

"What are you saying, Obed? You know Mother said we were not to talk with our mouths full!"

He started chewing very fast to allow himself to speak clearly.

"I said," he said loudly, "I'm glad Jakobi was able to bring his foot down and break the chalice on his first try. I want Ramani and his marriage to last a long, long time!"

---

‡ *"Seeker" - Judges 21*
* *Psalm 5:1-3 (para.)*

BARTIMAEUS

A Blind Man to Whom Jesus Gave Sight
Mark 10:46-52 and Luke 18:35-43

"He *is* your praise, and He *is* your God, who has done for you
these great and awesome things which your eyes have seen."
Deuteronomy 10:21 (NKJV)

BARTIMAEUS

Characters

Bartimaeus bar Timaeus (Bar-ti-ma-us)	Blind beggar
Ammi (Ahm-mee)	His female friend
Marcus Bentar (Mar-cus Ben-tar)	Ammi's father
Rebar (Ree-bar)	Ammi's deceased mother
Matthew (Mah-thew)	Ammi's eldest brother
Simon & Joseph	Ammi's twin brothers
Riyadah (Ree-yah-dah)	Ammi's older sister
Samuel (Sam-yu-el)	Ammi's first betrothed
Jesus (Jee-sus)	Teacher, Rabbi/Healer
Jonas (Joe-nahs)	Fellow beggar
Nathan (Na-than)	Fellow beggar
Eliud (El-ee-youd)	Synagogue priest/friend
Shemiah (Shem-i-yah)	Lead praise conductor
Shiloh Ziljan (Shy-lo Zil-jan)	Bartimaeus' first cousin
Azemi (Ah-zem-ee)	Cousin Ziljan's wife
Zerah, Eliel, (Ze-rah, El-ee-el)	Synagogue choir members
Aaron & Shimea (Ay-run, Shim-ee-a)	and Kohathite singers
Chion (Shee-on)	Ammi's Ethiopian servant
Retha (Ree-tha)	Bartimaeus' servant
Simeon (Sim-ee-on)	Retha's husband

† *Bris - Ceremony and celebration of circumcision performed by a priest/ mohel (professional specially trained in circumcision) to welcomes the male infant with the words: Baruch Ha-Ba. This means "blessed is the one who has arrived."*

Eryusin – *Definition: A separation period of the betrothed couple between 6-12 months prior to the wedding*

1

"He's too loud, entirely too loud!" the woman fumed to her two friends. "For once I would love to walk out of the synagogue and not have to hear that man's warbling!"

As they walked toward the city from the synagogue, the three women discussed the singing man sitting outside the building by the road begging alms and loudly singing.

Bartimaeus was one of the younger men by the gates. He was a handsome young man with a headful of dark brown curly hair, a small beard in need of trimming, a strong jaw line, and clouded eyes that stared straight ahead —for he was blind.

"I once heard that people who don't hear very well tend to speak and sing louder than normal," said one of the three women.

But her response was, "Bartimaeus can't see, however, he hears perfectly well. He's just irritating! After hearing a wonderful service and music by the priests, I certainly don't want to hear Blind Bartimaeus' stupid warbling!"

The two other women looked at each other but did not say anything in reply for they felt Bartimaeus had a lovely voice. After their friends' remarks they turned right and all three walked to the far side of the synagogue.

Bartimaeus sat tapping his stick to the music to which he was singing. Today he loudly sang a hymn he had heard earlier in the day in front of the outer courts of the synagogue. He was not allowed in the inner courts because of his infirmity of blindness, but sitting in the outer court with the infirmed still allowed him to hear the priests as they intoned the Word of the Lord to the people.

The high priest led a beautiful service and he was grateful to be in an area where he could hear everything that took place. He enjoyed the scriptures but his favorite part of the service was the singing – especially the songs where the congregation joined in.

He could hear the priests as they sang the words, followed by the people chiming in, then the cymbals, drums and horns. Some words were repetitious and Bartimaeus would add his voice while smiling toward the open arches of the synagogue.

The high holy services were his favorite for the singing would last a greater while.

Unbeknownst to Bartimaeus, many times the synagogue's musicians and priests were known to stand under the arches and listen to him. If they chanced to walk outside while he was singing, they would, at times, join with him and harmonize. When this happened, Bartimaeus would happily throw his head back in jubilation and rejoice while singing with them.

The beggars felt these were times when they felt as if they were actually inside the inner courts of the synagogue instead of outside by the gates.

Although he was blind, a few of the older townspeople who knew Bartimaeus' family history were aware of the blind singer's background and his Kohathite heritage. Many understood his need to sing.

The Kohathites were designated as singers under Asaph to lead worship in the temple at Jerusalem. Following the completion of the magnificent Temple by King Solomon, those singers were one of the four main divisions of the tribe of Levi who served as priests. They were known for their musical abilities – horns, drums, cymbals and the many stringed instruments.

Bartimaeus knew of his heritage at an early age, even though his father only sang around the home, whereas his mother loved to sing. She felt it was unfair that women were not allowed to join in the synagogue choirs. From the time he was able to comprehend the importance of music in the temple services, he made sure he was around the synagogue early enough to sit close in an area where he could hear.

The Lord may have allowed his blindness, but he felt the Lord had also gifted him with his voice and he vowed to always use it in praise to the Lord.

Along with his two best friends, Nathan and Jonas, Bartimaeus would tap his cane to set the pace and begin singing and the others would join in. Although his friends were not of the priestly tribe, they also enjoyed singing the various songs.

After all, Bartimaeus' singing meant more coins in their cups.

Many times small children and their parents would gather around him and he would teach them the words to the songs. There were also times when a crowd of adults would stand around and sing with them as Bartimaeus sang the loudest. The adults would often give him alms for there were those who enjoyed his tenor voice. When a popular and joyous song was sung, both he and his audience would tend to sing a bit louder than usual.

Then there were those who did not like hearing his singing, as was today. He was sitting next to other infirmed people near the city's pool outside the synagogue and decided to sing, even though services ended hours ago.

He remembered his mother singing around the house when he was a child. If she was not singing, she was humming a pleasant song. When she would put him to bed, she would kiss his forehead and rub one of his ears as she hummed him to sleep. Some things you never forget, he thought.

One of his mother's favorite sayings was, "Let everyone and everything that has breath and life praise the Lord, my son. That is why we are here!"

2

However, today was a good day for collecting alms, for he could hear the coins clinking in his cup as the townspeople contributed their coins to his and others' cups as they congregated at the gates. Not only were the coins in his cup clinking, but he could hear the clinking of coins in the cups of his friends sitting nearby.

Whenever Bartimaeus knew of crowds approaching, he would begin singing many of the special songs he knew people enjoyed, encouraging the people to drop coins in his cup as well as also dropping coins in the cups and bowls of those begging alms sitting nearby. The other infirmed knew a lot of their alms were given because of their friend's singing.

Comments of thanks were being said today and he smiled as he heard the coins clinking.

"Thank you, Bartimaeus!"

"That's one of my favorite songs."

"You sing it so well!"

"Beautiful singing, young man."

Those sitting with him who possessed sight would advise him when the crowd became larger. "More people are coming our way Bartimaeus, so sing another song!" And he always complied.

"Keep singing my friend," his friend Jonas said as he shook the coins in his small cup. As the people passed by the beggar section, those sitting nearby were happy to receive coins and egged him on.

Bartimaeus was happy to hear his friends receiving alms. Although he was not sure how much each was receiving, he knew the coins were more than they previously had in their cups and bowls. It was always good to hear their thanks and once again he tapped his stick for a new song and began singing an older hymn of praise.

As people hailed to him and the others their greetings, he waved his hands and continued to sing. He could feel that there was an air of expectation; he could feel anticipation in the air and that something good would happen today. His senses were very acute to the various atmospheres around him.

* * *

God is truly good, he thought, and life is good. What more could he ask for? He really had no regrets about his singing, even though others complained. He had learned to ignore negative voices and enjoy the positive.

Yet, Bartimaeus did have one regret: He could not see.

He wished to see at least one more time before he died. He would like to know what the sky looked like – was it still blue with white clouds? How green was grass? Were there flowers in the square, and if so, what color? What type? Was water as clear as he remembered? Were the stars still shining in the night sky? Were the gates to the Temple in Jerusalem still made of cedar?

He believed he might be an older brother to two babies, but they may have died in childbirth or from an illness for there were two deadly illnesses going around and many people died, but he was not sure. His parents had passed away when he was around 14 or 15 years of age. This was during the time he began to beg alms and lost contact with other relatives.

He knew his father's brother was overseeing his father's properties but neither he nor his family lived in Bartimaeus' family home. His father had purchased a small house for his son near the synagogue's gates, giving him some place to live that would place him closer to the synagogue. The home once belonged to one of his father's older friends who had since passed on.

He went home each night by counting his steps and rarely bumped into anything. Most of the townspeople knew he was blind and would step aside. Sometimes the children would lead him to his home as they sang along with him.

3

He had many friends and was called "Blind Bartimaeus" first by Eliud the priest to distinguish him from others with the name 'Bartimaeus' and the name was soon taken up by the other priests and eventually the townspeople.

Whenever he was down in spirit, Eliud would come out of the synagogue and make a point of talking with him and the other beggars to lift their spirits. He always knew that if Bartimaeus was not singing, something was wrong.

Bartimaeus did not beg alms as other blind citizens, but would put a bowl or cup near him in the event someone wanted to contribute funds toward his and others' living expenses — for beggars lived off the alms that were given them. His two closest friends had no place to live and refused to go to his house, but during the rains would enter into abandoned houses, or make their way to a nearby doorway until the storm passed. There were times when the priests would allow them to rest near the columns of the synagogue as long as it was not time for a service.

Bartimaeus had a small house that he lived in near the synagogue. It was very tiny and just the right size for him. Few knew of its whereabouts even though it was not a secret. Many children knew because they would sometimes walk beside him as he headed home.

He would share much of his proceeds with the other infirmed who begged alms near the synagogue, making sure no one would go hungry. Even though he was blind, he still had compassion on those less fortunate, and because of his singing would sometimes receive a nice collection of contributions and share his proceeds.

Each month he was to receive money from a trust his father had set up for him when he first became blind but seldom asked for any of it. His friends did not know of his background because they were all either infirmed or ill and, besides, it was not important to them. His uncle controlled the funds and distributed it as Bartimaeus had need, but Bartimaeus seldom required it.

Uncle Ziljan also taught his nephew how to feel the coins in order to know the denominations and be able to count. Bartimaeus knew the feel of various coins and was able to pay his tithes to the synagogue as well as the Roman taxes.

Lately, the Romans had started making different coins and he made a point of asking his childhood playmate and good friend, Ammi, what each one represented as well as what type of markings were on the face and back of the coins.

When he was a young child, he had normal sight, but a fall at the age of eight or nine rendered him blind. His parents had taken him to visit many doctors, but the prognosis was always the same: He would never regain his sight.

He still had dreams where he could see the stars, moon and sun. However, his main fear was that as he aged, he could no longer remember distinct colors. Blues, reds, greens and others were fading. Now he saw grays, blacks and light browns in his mind's eye and this bothered him. Would distinct colors go completely away? Plant colors were becoming plain colors and no longer resembled them as he remembered them when he was a seeing youngster. However, he thanked the Good Lord that his sense of touch was still working. His fingers could still identify materials of roughness and smoothness.

Even faces of people tended to blur in his mind although he remembered many by name. It was his prayer that the vagueness or distinctiveness would return. His dreams contained a lot of his memories and he did not want to let them go.

Although he vaguely remembered his parents' faces, he always remembered their voices – his mother's voice was loving and soft; his father's voice of a low manly timbre, but quiet. He was able to sense love, compassion, joy, sadness and happiness from the many voices of the people who walked past him. But he was also able to distinguish anger, hatred and jealousy.

Bartimaeus' hearing was very acute and he could distinguish many sounds that others could not hear or were ignored. Footsteps and animal sounds were able to peak his interest as they walked past him.

As the three women passed by making their comments he knew they, and others like them, did not appreciate his singing. As a teen, he began ignoring negative remarks against him and his infirmed friends.

Although he ignored them, Bartimaeus still did not like such remarks. He always felt the Lord enjoyed his praise and worship, even if he was not inside the synagogue. Just because he was blind did not mean he was not appreciative of what the Lord has been doing for him.

His mother had always said there is something good in every situation because the Lord knows every situation and He is good! If Bartimaeus thought of his mother too long, he would feel a bit sad, but he was always grateful for his many friends. He knew their friendship was honest and he did not have to worry about any deceptions.

4

His friend, Ammi, was his angel who had earlier taken the time to come by with a sandwich of barley bread and goat cheese, figs and a few dates, with a small closed gourd of water. He planned to eat half and save the rest for lunch. Earlier, the children had brought him a bunch of grapes and dark bread and he had eaten such fare for his morning meal.

He and Ammi were raised in the same neighborhood and played games together, even though she was almost two years younger. Of all his childhood friends, Ammi still took the time to visit with him and give him news of their families and friends. He was aware of people who moved away or those who died. She would sometimes bring food or water to him if she felt he didn't have any and even volunteered to run a few errands for him without being asked.

Ammi was beautiful when she was younger, and he believed she was still beautiful and her voice was soft and friendly. He remembered she had large expressive eyes and was always optimistic. She was of a compassionate nature and her steps were soft but sure. She had a tinkling laugh and when she was sad, she tried to camouflage it when she visited with him.

At the age of 14 or so, she had been betrothed to a man by the name of Samuel, who passed away over two years ago from an illness, prior to setting the date of her marriage.

Samuel was a handsome young man who was raised with wealth. He tended to sound haughty; so much so that even Bartimaeus' friends who sat with him pointed this out.

Bartimaeus could always feel Samuel's disdain whenever he accompanied Ammi and her family to the synagogue. Ammi always chose to converse with all of the men at the gates. He had once heard her tell Samuel of her friendship with Bartimaeus and how they were raised in the same area. He could tell that Samuel did not care to hear such comments from his betrothed and would change the subject. He could feel Ammi's girlfriends slowly separate themselves when Samuel was with her. He realized they were not fond of him either.

To be honest, Bartimaeus felt he would not want to hear about another man from his betroth's lips either. He realized, in his condition, he would not have to worry about being betrothed. He did not know of any of the infirmed men who sat with him being betrothed or if any of them even thought about marriage at all.

After the betrothal ceremony, the couple had little contact, for they were observing the *eryusin* period. During this time, Samuel became very ill. His father had to annul the betrothal contract when his son was near death and did not look as if he would recover. It wasn't long afterward that Samuel died.

Bartimaeus heard Ammi wore mourning clothes for almost a year, although Ammi explained she did so only out of respect for the young man's family. She was saddened by his death, but privately told him her betrothed seemed to be very nice; however, he was her parents' choice. Ammi only accepted him because her parents and brothers chose him, yet she barely knew him and prior to meeting him, had only seen him from afar with her brother, Matthew – and that not more than two or three times.

Samuel was one of her elder brother's friends and she had seen him as he and his father visited their home, yet she knew very little of his character and had not really interacted with him.

On the advice of her three brothers, her father was now allowing her to participate in the choosing of a husband, allowing her input into the next betrothal choice. Normally this was not done in the Jewish community. If the woman and man knew each other previous to the betrothal, all the better. Many never me their betrothed until just before the wedding.

She lately admitted to her father she had not found anyone with whom she wanted to spend the rest of her life. As she was getting older, she knew a decision had to be made soon. Her father told her he had been receiving requests from families for their sons to be included as suitors. Earlier her father had explained to prospective suitors that he wanted to make sure there was security for his youngest daughter. At Ammi's request, he had only allowed certain young men to court.

She knew her father felt love was secondary in a marriage, for security was first, but he loved his daughters. Ammi had an older sister, Riyadah, who had married well a few years ago and she was now pregnant with their first child. After seeing how happy her sister was with her husband, she knew that was what she wanted in a marriage. But Riyadah had known her husband prior to the betrothal and was happy he had been her father's choice.

5

Over the past few months of listening to the rumors of passersby, Bartimaeus and others with him had been aware that Jesus of Nazareth, the much talked-about teacher and healer, and the dozen men with whom He traveled, were visiting many of the cities in and around Galilee.

He recently heard that Jesus was approaching Jericho and perhaps would pass his way.

"Wouldn't it be nice for Jesus to come by and heal everyone who sat at the gate?" questioned those near him who begged alms. The Rabbi from Nazareth was known to heal all who came to him.

During mid-afternoon a few days later, a large crowd passed by the gates. His friend, Ammi, stopped by and excitedly stood near him. He could hear that she was rocking from one foot to the other.

"Bartimaeus, oh Bartimaeus, Jesus is coming this way! The Healer from Nazareth; remember, we talked about Him the other day! I have just heard that He recently healed a young man who was demon possessed in another town. He has healed others, perhaps He can restore your sight!"

At first Bartimaeus became hopeful, then put his head down. "Sure, Ammi, but the doctors have said that there is no hope for my sight to return. They believe something in my head must be hindering my healing. If it is possible to see again, it would surely be a miracle."

"Of course it would be a miracle, Bartimaeus! It was a miracle that the healing of a demon-possessed man took place. Our God works through men like this Rabbi. I know there have been others who claimed to be the Messiah, but the more I hear of this man, the more I believe He is the Messiah! Those other charlatans were never able to heal anyone and they did not teach as one with authority. You must have faith!"

Bartimaeus smiled at his friend. "I really want to hear Jesus' teachings because it is said that He speaks as a high priest and talks about the Kingdom of God. I've been hearing that from a lot of people who have seen and heard Him speak. It is said that He doesn't just drone on and on as some of our priests in the synagogue seem to do, but makes the love of the Father very plain so that everyone understands the scriptures."

But to see again. He had not considered that aspect.

"Ammi," he started, "do you believe Jesus could give me my sight back? The doctors could not do it when I was younger, and they still give me no hope today. I have been blind for such a long time...." His voice trailed off as he contemplated a healing by the Rabbi.

Ammi looked down at him as he sat close to the gate. She sensed her smile and lifted his head.

"I believe He can do it, just from what I've heard about Him," she quietly responded.

"If you believe it is possible, then so do I!" he declared.

"Jesus has cleansed lepers and healed others. I know He can heal you!"

Ammi looked around and realized that time was fleeting. "I have to go or my brothers will come looking for me. I promise I'll be back later in the day."

He knew when she left because her pleasant aroma began to dissipate. He also knew her brothers were not in agreement with their friendship for he had grown into a man and a young woman of her age and heritage was supposed to be careful around men. His friends had recently mentioned to him it was time for her to start wearing a veil for she was very comely; even now she should be properly chaperoned.

Ammi's mother had died of the same illness as his parents, and while her brothers were never far from their sister for she was of marriageable age, he agreed she should have a proper chaperone. Her three brothers knew of her fondness for Blind Bartimaeus and this worried her family.

He knew if he had his sight things would have been different. His family and Ammi's family had been great friends when he was younger, but his loss of sight and his parents' deaths changed everything.

6

Jonas and Nathan had been listening to their friend's conversation with Ammi. They talked among themselves about Jesus' arrival in Jericho. They knew they were sitting in an area where Jesus may not walk.

"Bartimaeus and Jonas," began Nathan, "let's walk closer to an area where Jesus may pass by. If we stay here, we may never see Him. If this Rabbi has the power to heal the sick and lame, perhaps He will strengthen my legs, heal Jonas' back and allow you to see again. I would love for my legs to become straight and be able to walk on my own like other people and I believe this Man is able to do it. Even if He doesn't, we might still be able to hear Him teach."

At Nathan's remarks, the other two hesitated and then all three picked up their cups and stood. With Nathan holding on to the other men's shoulders, all began heading toward the road leading into Jericho. Some of the children of the town saw Bartimaeus and his friends and began walking behind the three men as they laughed and sang some of their favorite childhood songs.

Jonas and Nathan soon tired and decided to sit on two of the large boulders by the side of the road. The singing children decided to stay with Bartimaeus who led them into some of the songs he remembered as a child.

Bartimaeus continued to walk and joke with the children and when they halted, the children informed him that he was on the Jericho Road. They led him to a large stone wall and he proceeded to position himself as he sat there with his cup by his side. The children said goodbye to him and laughing merrily continued to run in the direction of the crowd to catch up with their families. People traveling on the road saw the cup and began to drop in a few coins. Smiling, he hummed to himself and when he heard a crowd of people passing by, he tried to find out what was taking place.

When he questioned the people, some ignored him, but a few stopped by to tell him that Jesus from Nazareth was coming that way.

"There are crowds of people surrounding him, Bartimaeus, including twelve men, whom we all believe are Jesus' disciples." His informer patted him on the back and left him.

The crowd was getting noisier, so he believed Jesus must be very close.

At this realization, Bartimaeus began shouting, "Jesus, son of David, have mercy on me!" He raised his voice as the rabble of the crowd came closer, and cried out again, "Jesus, son of David, please have mercy on me, a blind man!"

The people tried to shush him. "That's Blind Bartimaeus. Someone should tell him to be quiet!"

At this, he ignored the comments and began to shout much louder, knowing Jesus might not hear him for the noisy crowd around him. He decided to become brave because he was on a quest. This might be his only chance to see if it was possible to be healed. As he could hear the people's footsteps were very close, he continued to shout, "Jesus, son of David, have mercy on me."

"Shut up, Bartimaeus! Jesus has no time for you." Such remarks only made him more brave and shout even louder.

All he could think was, "I must be persistent and try my best to get the Healer's attention!" So he continued to shout at the top of his lungs. Without the children to guide him, he was not sure how close he was to the Healer and His disciples.

Soon the shuffling footsteps stopped and the many voices were beginning to cease. He wondered what was happening, but decided that Jesus would be able to hear him much better without so much noise and continued to shout.

He heard a Voice say kindly to someone, "Call that man and have him come to me."

Soon he heard, "The Rabbi wants the blind man to come to him." "He wants the blind man." Those same words were being whispered repeatedly around him.

Close by he heard a woman's voice speaking to someone in the crowd, "The Rabbi is saying someone should bring the shouting man to Him."

Movement began as someone came through the crowd on Jesus' request. He thought the person must be important because he could feel the crowd separating as someone moved toward him.

Was the Voice… was it the Rabbi? Did he hear Jesus' voice? Even over the rabble, he was able to hear Jesus speaking to the people around him. He heard footsteps coming closer and not sure of what was happening, shouted once more, "Jesus, please have mercy on me!"

Then he felt someone tap his shoulder and he heard his friend, Eliud the priest, say, "Cheer up, Bartimaeus! The Rabbi is calling for you. "Come, my friend, leave your stick and follow me; we will go toward Him together." Bartimaeus felt along the boulder and leaned the stick along its side and nervously walked with Eliud.

Eliud took hold of his elbow and led him forward. It did not take long for the priest to have him standing directly in front of Jesus.

7

As he moved forward, brave Blind Bartimaeus was now the "not-so-brave" Blind Bartimaeus. His knees shook and Eliud could feel the quivering of his friend's arm muscles.

The Voice asked him, "What is your request? What would you have me do for you?"

Bartimaeus' heart stopped and after a few seconds he could feel it begin to beat loudly and quickly in his chest, for he was then at a loss for words. He bowed his head, swallowing quickly, until he felt he could speak again.

Quietly he said, "My Lord, I believe you possess heavenly powers and are able to heal me." He hesitated a few seconds and then continued. "I would like to regain my sight – I would like to see once again."

There was a slight hush as the crowd around him quieted in order to hear the Rabbi's response to his request. Jesus looked upon the now silent crowd, knowing they expected a miracle. He did not move closer to the blind man, for there was no reason to touch him.

There was a feeling of expectancy in the air. Once again Jesus slowly smiled at the crowd.

Looking deep into Bartimaeus' eyes, He said, "In that case, young man, receive your sight, for your faith has made you well."

Immediately there was a slight warmth in his forehead as Bartimaeus' vision began to blur and slowly clear. The crowd moved even closer around the two men and held their breath, waiting. Suddenly colors burst in his sight with clarity. Within seconds he could see people standing on both sides of a Man he immediately knew was Jesus the Healer.

Eliud was still standing beside Bartimaeus and looked into his face. He noticed the cloudy look in his friend's eyes seemed to slowly disappear.

Bartimaeus' new sight took in the Rabbi's face, hair, height, his robe and clear eyes. He knew he would never forget the face, eyes, or Voice of the Man who had healed him.

"I can see, I can see!" He whispered and began to cry as the people reacted to his announcement. He slowly turned his head from one side to the other as he scanned the people staring at him, noticing that many were smiling, but even more were crying.

Bartimaeus began praising God, crying and lifting his hands high. "Thank you, Jesus, thank you! Praise God! Praise Him for sending You!"

Those nearest Jesus began to spread the word to those at the back of the crowd. "He can see! He's healed! Bartimaeus can see!"

The people stopped to listen as Bartimaeus threw his head back and began singing in his most beautiful voice the psalm he'd recently heard at the last praise service in the synagogue:

"Praise the LORD! Oh praise the LORD from the heavens; praise him in the heights; praise him all his angels; praise him, all his hosts. Praise him sun and moon; praise him all stars of light. Praise him heavens of heavens, and waters that are above the heavens.

Let everyone praise the name of the LORD: for he commanded, and they were created. He has also established them for ever and ever. He has made a decree which shall not pass. Praise the LORD from the earth all dragons, and all deeps. Fire and hail, snow and vapors, stormy wind fulfilling his word; mountains, and all hills; fruitful trees, and all cedars; beasts, and all cattle; creeping things, and flying fowl.

Kings of the earth, and all people -- princes, and all judges of the earth -- both young men, and maidens; old men, and children.

Let them praise the name of the LORD, for his name alone is excellent; His glory is above the earth and heaven. He also exalts the horn of his people, the praise of all His saints; even of the children of Israel, who are a people near and dear unto Him.

Oh praise the LORD!" *

All the people heard him and were amazed. Most began to applaud as he sang. Many of the nearby priests joined in as Jesus closed His eyes while giving a pleased smile. With Bartimaeus in the lead and the priests swelling the end of the psalm, all the people gave praise for the miracle, while loudly repeating "God is good! God is good!"

Bartimaeus had always been a wonderful singer, but today he now sang as never before. Many began clapping their hands and praising God along with Bartimaeus. Some slapped his back in joy and others rejoiced and applauded.

Jesus nodded his head at Bartimaeus and smiled as He turned, said something to one of the men behind him, and then continued his trek down the road.

Once again, the crowd followed.

---

*Psalm 148 (para.)

8

Turning his head, Bartimaeus noticed the smiling young man similar to his age and height in a flowing dark robe and a small embroidered yarmulke on his head.

Standing in front of him and putting his arms around Bartimaeus, he joyously spoke one word: "Miracle!"

Right away, he knew. Eliud! For the first time, he was looking at Eliud the priest, who was his friend and who led him toward the Healer -- they smiled at one another and then, without hesitation, hugged.

He vaguely remembered his friend as a young boy, slightly older than himself. He recalled that Eliud had lived in his area, but attended synagogue school following his bar mitzvah.

Eliud released his friend, turned and gave a small wave as he quietly said, "I hope to see you soon in service at the synagogue, Bartimaeus — in the inner courts!" and began walking to the side of the twelve men who traveled with Jesus, joining with the multitude of people who followed.

Bartimaeus realized that he would now be able to go into the inner courts of the synagogue with other men.

He remained on the road as people filed past him. Many of the women hugged him and men shook his hand, but he was still stunned as the crowd continued to follow the Rabbi. He continued to stand in the same spot where he was healed.

Lifting his head, he squinted upward and saw a yellow sun and a blue sky with white clouds. His memory of colors returned and he continued to sob as he looked around the area, seeing small plants, trees, rocks, and items he remembered from his childhood. Green, brown, orange, white – each color within another color spread over the earth. Falling to his knees, he continued to bless the Lord in praise and thanksgiving.

Looking up, he saw a figure approaching and immediately recognized Ammi coming toward him holding a small bag, which he knew contained something for him to eat. There was a huge smile on her face. She was no longer a child, but still the same beautiful young girl in his memory. She had not changed very much from his last glimpse of her as a child – of course taller, more mature, with thick silky brown hair in a long braid down her back and tears in her beautiful brown eyes. The scarf she wore on her head was a mixture of colors which made her eyes shine with tears.

He began to stand as she put her left hand on his right shoulder and both began to silently cry. "You look the same as when we were very young – but lovelier."

Embarrassed, she blushed as he made the remark and quickly turned her face from him.

"I can see, Ammi! I can see!" He smiled down at her as he looked into her eyes. "You were so right. The Rabbi did not even touch me, but only looked at me and proclaimed me healed. I had given up hope, but the more I shouted to Him, I felt something in my spirit and knew right then He would be able to give me my sight. Your faith in Jesus gave me new hope and strengthened my own faith."

Ammi was so overwhelmed, she could not speak. She only nodded while searching his eyes. Bartimaeus' eyes, which were once set and a bit cloudy, were now a very clear dark brown and he was blinking normally.

They conversed for a short time and soon it was time for Ammi to return home, for it was approaching mealtime. Silently she gave a great hug to Bartimaeus and left him as both began to head in separate directions.

9

Bartimaeus started for his small home by counting the steps. He chuckled to himself as he realized he would no longer have to do so. He slowly walked while looking around at the busy townspeople, various homes, gardens, and marketplaces with traders, and identifying people he normally knew only by their voices.

He noticed the style of dress had not changed much over the years, except the colors seemed to be brighter than he remembered. The men walked in the same manner and the women chatted in groups as they used to do when his mother was alive.

Previously he utilized his nose to identify the traders' areas, animal stalls, the bakers' and vegetable sellers' areas. He stopped to greet people and repeatedly testified of his healing by Jesus the Healer while receiving many hugs, kisses, and tears from neighbors and friends.

The children who had previously walked with him toward the Jericho Road, now walked beside him. They were as jubilant as he. One little girl asked him to stand by a tree and bend down so she could look into his eyes.

"I love you, Bartimaeus, and I'm glad you can now see what I look like!"

He hugged her and patted the others on their heads, thanking them for their help. "Now I know what each of you looks like," he answered. The children laughed and waved at him as they turned to the left road.

Reaching his small home, he immediately noticed the clutter inside and decided that after washing and changing his clothes he would start clearing his three small rooms.

Placing his old walking stick against the wall, he murmured to himself, "I'm a new man."

Bartimaeus looked into the package that Ammi had brought him and found large portions of fruit, goat cheese, dark bread and pieces of broiled fish. He sat at his small table and began to eat, slowly chewing and savoring every bite while drinking water out of the same cup he had been using to beg alms.

When he had dipped his cup into the bucket of water that was kept beside his door, he calmly watched as the water rippled around the bucket. "How beautiful," he sighed.

Looking into a small reflective plate, he began to study his face and hands. He noticed the lines on his hands and his dirty fingernails, as well as the small shaggy beard on his chin. Picking up a sharp instrument, he began cutting the hair of his beard from his jaw line to his chin. He tried to cut his beard in a shape he saw on the men he passed on the road.

"I'll have to learn how to trim my beard correctly," was his first thought.

He washed himself all over, being careful to scrub his fingers extra hard to clean his fingernails, and changed into clean clothing. For the first time, he wondered how he had always appeared to Ammi before he could see what he really looked like. She'll never see me looking that way again, he thought. He began talking to himself, making plans for the rest of the day.

"Now I will go to the synagogue for the proclamation of healing and offer a sacrifice. Then I will try to see if Jesus is still in Jericho."

He looked up as he noticed shadows of two men standing outside his entryway. As he walked toward the door, a joyful Jonas and Nathan entered. Jonas was standing straight and tall and Nathan no longer needed his makeshift crutch, for his legs were no longer twisted.

Bartimaeus stared at his two friends as they stared back at him. Then all three began hugging one another and crying. It seems Jesus had passed them by as well and they, too, had screamed for Jesus to have mercy on them.

"He didn't even touch us," sobbed Jonas, "He told us our sins were forgiven, and continued walking. We had heard you shouting, so when He came closer, we began shouting, 'Jesus have mercy on us.' We did the same as He came near to where we were. And He heard us!"

Nathan was literally bouncing, he was so happy. "We heard from the townspeople that you had been healed also. The children led us here for we wanted to hurry to your home as fast as we could."

Smiling, Bartimaeus told of his healing. "He did not touch me either. Eliud led me toward Him and I plan to return to the synagogue to offer a sacrifice for my healing. Come with me, my friends. Let's go get our sacrifices for the priests." Both men nodded.

He shared his remaining food and quickly found clean robes for them. As Jonas and Nathan washed, they discussed purchasing two doves apiece for sacrifice.

"Do you know," pondered Nathan, "we received more than enough alms from the people who passed us by than we have all week sitting at the gate. I believe Jesus had a hand in that, for after He healed us, He told us to show ourselves to the priests, then He walked away. Right away, people began throwing coins into our cups. I don't know how, but I believe it was to make sure that we would have enough for a sacrifice at the synagogue for our healing. It just seems strange that all of a sudden we had more than enough."

The others agreed and all three began to praise the Lord for their healing and for sending Jesus to Jericho.

Since Nathan and Jonas generally slept in the open, Bartimaeus offered his home to his friends.

"I've made the decision to return to my family's home which has been empty for some time, but you two are more than welcome to remain here. I will remove only a few personal items to make myself comfortable because I have not been to the place where I grew up in many years. My father's brother has been handling my family's business matters and perhaps knows where members of my family might be located."

As his friends joyfully accepted his offer, they again discussed their health since being healed and what they planned for their futures.

"Now that you can see, my friend, have you noticed how beautiful Ammi looks?" Jonas slyly looked at Bartimaeus and winked. Nathan gave a broad smile and both men gave a few chuckles. The conversation then shifted to their thoughts concerning their immediate futures.

"As for myself," Jonas continued, "I plan to return to my village and perhaps find a nice wife for myself. There are many beautiful widows in Jericho and since I'm no longer infirmed, a few of them approached me as we walked here. I never noticed them and I'm quite sure they never noticed me before when I sat outside the synagogue, but it sure feels good knowing that women still find me somewhat attractive."

Nathan quietly pondered his own thoughts. "You should think about marrying and having children, my friend. Unlike us, you're a young man and should not grow old alone. If you remember, Ammi's family is allowing her input in choosing her next betrothed. The other one, the rich one — wasn't his name Samuel or something like that? — died of an illness or something – isn't that right Jonas?" His friend gave a nod.

"Ammi's not getting any younger and may feel compelled to accept someone soon or her father will betroth her. Remember, my friend, she has brothers who have more male friends they might suggest to help her make a decision."

Bartimaeus blushed, but refused to respond. "Come, my friends. Let's prepare to visit the synagogue for the evening prayers. We will be able to see the priests at that time."

The three men headed for the door, with Bartimaeus in the lead.

Following a visit to the area where sacrificial animals were sold, Bartimaeus, Jonas and Nathan brought their doves to the priests and, following the sacrifices, acknowledged their healings. Right after the giving of sacrifices, all were directed by the priests to the male area of the synagogue for the evening services. They were pleased to note that the songs for the service were songs they all knew.

Their first service inside the synagogue was something they would always hold in their hearts. First their amazing healings and then the opportunity to go into the inner courts for service. This was a wonderful spiritual experience. They sat together and recited their prayers in unison.

With tears running down their cheeks, all three thought, "God is so good!"

10

Every chance they were able, the three men traveled to hear Jesus as He taught the people; sometimes behind the synagogue, sometimes in the square, and many times on the hillsides. They enjoyed listening to his resonant voice and how he explained the Kingdom of God. Bartimaeus always made sure they were situated where he and his friends could see and hear Jesus. This was no problem for when Jesus taught in the hill areas outside of town where his voice would carry, all the people had great seats.

They also attended services in the town's synagogue. Bartimaeus' beautiful voice blended well with the priests and when the prayers were over they would leave the synagogue together.

One evening, as they prepared to leave following the praise, Bartimaeus thought he heard someone calling his name but saw no one.

By the time the men reached the first exit arch, Bartimaeus' friend, Eliud, ran to catch up with them. "Bartimaeus, my friend, it is so good to see you during prayers. I have been trying to catch you before you left the building and today I have been successful. Please come with me to the priests' area. I and my friends have a request."

Jonas and Nathan greeted Eliud and said they would meet Bartimaeus at his house later in the evening. Nathan said he and Jonas had met many new friends in the synagogue and would go visit with them for awhile.

Eliud led Bartimaeus to another area of the synagogue into a large open section in the rear. As they walked into the hall, he looked into the faces of at least 75 or more men. A tall older priest with a brightly colored yarmulke approached them and bowed before Bartimaeus.

"You are no longer blind, is that so, Bartimaeus?" It was more of a statement than a question and Bartimaeus gave a wide grin.

"No, my lord," he answered.

The priest smiled in return. "I am happy to hear that. You see, we have been hearing your voice for many years and I have enjoyed your singing. I have checked into your background and find that you are of the order of Kohathites, who are of the tribe of Levi, whose son Gershom sets the order of priests from his father, Aaron, brother of Moses. I am Shemiah, lead conductor of praise music for the Lord Almighty."

Shemiah waved his left hand toward four men in the front section. "These are Zerah, Eliel, Aaron and Shimea, heads of the choirs. You already know Eliud, who is also a part of us. They and others with us would be pleased to have you join us for a short meeting."

"We are your brethren under our ancestors Asaph and Heman and are in charge of the opening and closing of the gates, serving as doorkeepers, keepers of the veil, and those who care for the instruments of praise. But most importantly, we conduct the music of the synagogue."

"We are all priests of the order of Kohathites and have been appointed through Moses as well as by King David to serve as singers, accompanied by instruments of music, namely those songs you heard this evening for the service of praise. We are in charge of the harps, stringed instruments, and cymbals, and the raising of our voices with resounding joy." **

"You, my son, sing with resounding joy and we would be pleased to offer you your rightful place as a Kohathite singer in the synagogue."

Bartimaeus was dumbfounded. To be able to sing in the synagogue was the most wonderful news he had ever heard and a blessed opportunity. To do something he really enjoyed was marvelous! He wanted to cry for this was an honor. If his father were alive, he knew he would be pleased to have a son who sang in the synagogue choirs.

"There is one problem that has presented itself and we must discuss it before you make your decision. What we discuss in this room and in the presence of these singers and musicians should stay here." Shemiah lifted one eyebrow as his eyes swept the room before continuing.

"We all know you were healed by Jesus, the Rabbi from Nazareth for we were in the crowd along with the multitude." Taking a long breath, he continued.

"There are many priests, including our Chief Priest, who are not in agreement with His teachings or how he purports himself to be the Son of God. However, we believe he is the Messiah, for we have not only seen the miracles He performs, but have studied the scrolls and prophecies with the scribes. We have also seen and heard how He teaches, heals, and performs miracles. Only a man sent from God can do what He does."

"Our question to you is this: How do you feel about the Rabbi –the Man, Jesus?"

Shemiah did not smile as he stood beside Eliud and the four priests while they awaited Bartimaeus' answer.

Bartimaeus looked at the six priests and without hesitation, gave his answer.

"I, too, know that only a man sent from God has the capacity to heal as He does. The prophets have declared that the Messiah will be born in Bethlehem-Ephrathah in Judea, and that is where Jesus was born. He has spoken that His purpose is not to change any of our Jewish laws and I feel His teachings tell us more about the character of our Heavenly Father. He does not teach like our priests or any of the scribes, Pharisees or Sadduccees."

"My answer is this: I, too, believe as you all do — that Jesus, the Teacher and Healer, is the long-awaited Messiah. And yes, I would like to become a part of my heritage!"

At this, all of the priests began shouting and praising God. Soon they all lifted their voices and beautifully sang a song of praise and thanks from the hymn of their ancestor Asaph, with Bartimaeus adding his voice to theirs.

"We praise you, oh God, we praise you, for your Name is near; people tell of your wonderful deeds. You say, I choose the appointed time; it is I who judge with equity. When the earth and all its people quake, it is I who hold its pillars firm; to the arrogant I say, 'Boast no more,' and to the wicked, 'Do not lift up your horns. Do not lift your horns against heaven; do not speak so defiantly.'"…

As for me, I will declare this forever; I will sing praise to the God of Jacob, who says, I will cut off the horns of all the wicked, but the horns of the righteous will be lifted up." #

Excerpts from Psalm 75 NIV

11

After renting a donkey and a small wagon, Bartimaeus slowly began moving a few of his personal items to his family's home on the outskirts of Jericho, leaving some of his furniture for his two friends. He had been living in his family's home for over a month and had recently received money from his trust fund in order to furnish some of the rooms more to his liking. He knew he would need a woman's touch if he wanted his house to look warm and inviting.

For the last couple of days he began contemplating marriage and children. As he visited the marketplace, he would see families shopping together or parents escorting their sons to the various Hebrew schools. He knew he wanted to have a family with many children.

His mind began to wander toward his own childhood when his parents were alive – how his father would put him on his shoulders as his mother shopped with the traders and at the marketplace. He also thought about Ammi, how they used to play together, and how beautiful she had become.

He remembered teasing her about her long hair and she would tell him how her brothers would also tease her, putting gooey items into her hair, for she was the baby girl; her much older sister had married a few years ago. Her long hair was now a beautiful dark brown color which flowed below her waist and glistened in the sun whenever she moved her head.

Giving a huge sigh, he grabbed his money bag and started for the shops nearby.

* * *

As he reached the door, a tall man stood in front of him and approached him with a faint smile on his face, asking if he was Gerar Bartimaeus bar Timaeus. Bartimaeus gave him a strange look, for the man looked quite a bit the way his late father looked when he last saw him.

This man was about six or seven years his senior but it had been years since anyone had spoken to him using his full name. No one called him Gerar, except his late mother. Gerar had been the name of her baby brother, who had died at an early age.

He nodded his head and cautiously answered in the affirmative.

"Bartimaeus, it is so good to meet you. My name is Shiloh Ziljan bar Timaeus." He waited while his name sank into Bartimaeus' brain.

Bartimaeus invited him inside and grabbed two stools so they could sit facing each other.

"Timaeus? My brother? You are one of my brothers?" He asked in surprise for he was unaware of an older brother.

The man looked a bit crestfallen. "No, I am sorry to tell you your two young brothers died at an early age, but I am your first cousin, Shiloh Ziljan. I am the son of your father's elder brother, Ziljan and live in the mountainous region of Idumea. I came to check on your father's holdings, a job my late father used to perform. Because you were infirm and your parents and brothers are dead, your property came to me as a portion inheritance over which I control."

He stood; Bartimaeus did the same. A relative! He grabbed his cousin and the two men hugged for some time.

"I had heard of the miracle of your healing and your ability to now see and had to come see you. You look more than well. I was not sure where you lived, since the last I heard was that you lived in town. When I visited your home by the synagogue, I found your two friends who were also healed and they directed me here. I was not in town during your healing, but have heard what happened and that you are now able to see."

"My father passed away over six months ago and the control of your trust fell to me as the firstborn male. Your father — my uncle — was wise in his investments of sheep and cattle and you, my cousin, are quite a wealthy man! As the eldest, and now the only son of your father, we need to discuss your inheritance."

The two men conversed for some time.

* * *

About that time, Bartimaeus heard a slight rustling at the door and looked up to see Ammi standing in the doorway. She was wearing a veil and looked wonderful.

"I presume this is your wife?" Ziljan asked as both men stood when she entered the doorway.

Ammi blushed and Bartimaeus gave a great grin. Without answering his question, Bartimaeus said, "I need to clean up a bit, for we are on our way to hear the Healer who is teaching on the outskirts of town. Afterwards I'll come to where you are staying to discuss my finances."

Ziljan gave directions to his rented house and started to hold out his hand. Then, without hesitation, both men grabbed each other and hugged. He bid both of them a good day and departed, saying he would have his servants prepare for an evening meal to entertain his cousin.

Jesus did not stay in the area for a long time, but whenever they knew he was near, Bartimaeus, Ammi, and the woman she called Chion, would travel to the hillsides where He was known to teach. Bartimaeus made a point of trying to memorize everything he heard during those occasions. His favorite messages were on the subject of the Kingdom of God. He knew there were those who felt Jesus should overthrow the Roman government and lead as the King of the Jews, but he quickly understood that the Kingdom to which Jesus was referring was located inside men's hearts.

One day Jesus passed by Bartimaeus and Ammi after having a teaching session with the crowd and stopped to touch Ammi's shoulder. He slowed His steps and looked her in the eyes. She smiled and as Jesus smiled in return, He put his other hand on Bartimaeus' shoulder, blessed the two of them and quietly said, "God is with you."

They looked at each other and then at the Rabbi's retreating back as he moved on.

12

Ammi was very quiet as Bartimaeus and her twin brothers headed the wagon toward her home. Bartimaeus was not sure if she was angry with him for not explaining to his cousin their relationship or if she was thinking of something else. As they walked together toward her house in silence, he began to worry about her feelings towards him.

At the entrance to her home, he finally asked her, "Have I made you angry, or did I do something wrong?"

"No," she turned toward him with sadness in her eyes. "Things have changed at my house since you are now able to see. My father and brothers feel it is not right for me to continue visiting your home without an escort. When my mother died, I was very young and they were somewhat lenient with me, but I'm older now. My elder brother has stressed that as young Jewish woman, I now need to wear a veil at all times and to become more circumspect. Previously they allowed me to come see you because we were friends and our meetings were always in an open area, but you and I are older and now you've moved to your family home. My younger brothers brought me to your house and, as you could see, came to bring me home."

"In the beginning, when you were blind, very little was said and my father always made sure one of my brothers or Chion was nearby. Since your sight has returned and you have moved to a home with no servants, I won't be able to visit you without one of my brothers or a chaperone to accompany me. Today is my last day being allowed to be alone with you even though I always request Chion to chaperone me. My brothers allowed me to be in your company today without a chaperone because we were around a lot of people."

"I had planned to tell you that earlier when I arrived, but your cousin was there. I am so sorry, Bartimaeus."

He could see she had been holding back tears and when he took her hands, her fingers trembled.

Bartimaeus had already given thought to the matter over the last few days and had planned to speak his thoughts with her later. As he climbed down from the little wagon, he hesitated.

"Don't worry, Ammi. In the meanwhile I will begin coming to see you at your house so that either your family, or chaperones and servants will be nearby. I had planned to speak to your father in the next day or so."

He wanted to console her, but decided now was not the time. Slowly he released her hands as they said their goodbyes. Bartimaeus watched her as she slowly followed her brothers and entered her home; he continued on his way to his cousin's rented house.

13

The meeting with Ziljan was very surprising to Bartimaeus. His cousin was in a nicely furnished rented house and he had brought a few servants with him. The meal was excellent and he commented that it was the best meal he had eaten in years. Ziljan's cook was pleased with his comments.

Ziljan pulled a flat shoulder bag toward him which contained many scrolls, papers and drawings as he began to relate to his cousin the amount of funds, property, and servants Bartimaeus had inherited. As he pulled out the documents, he began to point out the many items Bartimaeus owned which boggled his mind.

It seems his late father had made sure his son would be financially able to live independently after he first became blind. He and his brother had contacted a man of business in town who was known for his integrity and would make sure Bartimaeus would want for nothing. There was more than enough money to take care of a household, keep and hire servants, and support a future family for the rest of his life. As the years passed, the investments continued to grow under the trusteeship of Ziljan's father.

Ziljan explained the amounts of sheep, cattle, property and horses, and suggested Bartimaeus keep the servants and their families his late father had working for him, some of whom lived on the property and others who did not, for they would be as loyal to him as they were to his father.

"Servants are strange workers, Bartimaeus. If they are loyal, it is always better to have them remain with you. If they are not loyal, get rid of them and see if your loyal servants have families who share their same work ethics. Your father rarely removed servants from the household and most of them were family members. Keep that in mind, young man!"

A meeting was set up for two days' time so he and Bartimaeus could travel to meet his many shepherds, groomsmen, and the house and field servants who were already in place. There were a few older house servants that lived in the area, but were awaiting word to see if Bartimaeus would keep them and their families in their positions. Since no one had lived in his family's home for some time, a skeleton group of workers made sure the house was always secure and clean.

Bartimaeus thought for a few seconds and asked, "Ziljan, do you think there is any chance that my mother's housekeeper, cook, and the other house servants would be willing to retain their positions and come back as soon as possible? I may remember some of them from when I was young and still living at home. I would be very happy to meet with them."

"Ah ha," Ziljan laughed, "Are you tired of cooking and cleaning for yourself, my cousin? Of course, I have instructed them to report to you in two days' time. Your wife can give them instructions as to how she desires her household run. She may wish to have the servants purchase material to have new curtains and order new pottery. I'm not certain what happened to the old dishes, pottery and other cooking utensils, but you will need those extra items as you completely settle in."

"To help you become acclimated to your new-found wealth, I plan to stay in town for five to six weeks to advise you and introduce you to the man of business we've been using for your property and finances. You would be wise to continue to retain him in that position until you decide to choose another."

Bartimaeus nodded and said, "If you trust him, then he will stay with me."

"Good! I was hoping you would say that," said Ziljan. "He will make sure you learn bookkeeping skills for I'm not sure how far you were able to go in your studies before you lost your sight. He is honest and will give you the appropriate advice you and your wife will need. Of course, all decisions to be made will be up to you."

At this point, Bartimaeus decided it was time to explain his relationship with Ammi, how they were playmates as children and how her friendship and support through the years bonded them. He also mentioned the request of the Kohathite priests to be a singer at the synagogue.

"I really do love Ammi and want to marry her, but first I must speak with her family, especially her father. I don't know if he will allow me to wed his daughter. I understand he was in attendance at my healing, but I don't know if he sees me as other than Blind Bartimaeus, the beggar. He has always been friendly to me and was a friend of my parents, but I have not seen him since I received my sight."

Bartimaeus gave a great sigh. "I am not interested in Ammi's dowry, although her father is quite well-to-do. Even if her family was poor as a bag of old dates, I would still love her. When she was betrothed to another man, I was downhearted, but when he died prior to the wedding, she came to me for comfort. She told me she never loved him, but the betrothal contract had been sealed by both fathers and the wedding would have taken place later should he have lived."

"I don't want to lose her, Ziljan. I understand she has had other suitors, but her family is allowing her to have a say in choosing her next betrothed. I don't know how long they will wait to sign a contract. Ammi is my heart."

"Have you told her how you feel?" Ziljan cocked his head to the side as he looked his cousin in the face.

"No. I think it's because I don't know how she feels." Bartimaeus gave a deep sigh and put his face in his hands. He later removed them and sat back in his chair, while running his fingers through his hair.

"I started to tell her today when she informed me that her family wants her to stop visiting my house. I understood for I live alone in a large house with no servants to chaperone. Besides, I have been walking her home alone in the late evenings, which is not good for appearances. I really want to marry her."

"Do it, Bartimaeus!" Ziljan smiled. "It is wonderful to love the woman you marry and not have to go through the custom of being betrothed to someone you don't really know or love. I, too, grew up with my wife, Azemi, who is as beautiful as your Ammi. We have three healthy sons and two beautiful daughters. Already my eldest daughter has male friends who will later, I am sure, become suitors, for she is quickly becoming of marriageable age. I know that soon I will be scrutinizing all the young men who will want to speak for her."

"As your older cousin I will represent your late father and speak on your behalf to Ammi's family about your finances and the fact that you will be able to support her in a worthy manner. A man in your position needs a wife, as well as heirs. As my father once told me, 'rich men fare better with a chosen wife'."

"When my father told me that old saying, we both laughed about it for I thought he was making a joke. However, when many of the young girls in my city reached the age of betrothal, I was considered quite a catch — if I say so myself."

Ziljan's eyes sparkled as he reminisced. "I had at least three young women and their mamas visiting my mother every day, parading them into the house, thinking I would come through the room and make a declaration for one of them. I have never known whether my mother invited them or if they just happened to drop by. I began making myself scarce when I would see them heading toward our home."

"Once I was too late and my mother called me from my room to come greet the 'visitors'. I was taught to be polite, but as soon as I could, I would make like a horse and trot away. After that I made sure my mother did not see me before I left home. The servants knew what I was doing and would cover for me." At this he and Bartimaeus had a great laugh.

Bartimaeus averted his eyes as he thought. "Since I was blind, I had never considered that problem. No father wanted his daughter married to a blind man unless he became blind after marriage. When I think about it now, I never knew what any of the girls in town looked like. I barely remembered some who were in my age group. I could only recognize voices. Some voices were harsh or shrill and others were soft, but I did not care, for I felt marriage would never be in my future."

"I was just happy to have Ammi in my life for a time. I knew that eventually she would marry and no decent man would allow his wife to visit a man on her own, least of all a blind man who sat outside the synagogue. I was always afraid that her father would take the 'matchmaker' route and allow them to find her someone to wed."

Ziljan did not say anything, but tapped his finger on his chin. "When my daughters are old enough, I believe I will allow them to have some participation in the decision-making process for their future husbands. There are matchmakers where I live, and many Jewish people use them, but I think the couple should have some feelings for each other. It makes for a better union."

"Every man wants to make sure his daughter will be well taken care of in the future. There was no problem with my betrothal for when I told my father I wished to marry Azemi, he was very pleased. And when my father went to her father, her family, especially her mother, was very receptive and pleased also, for our families were friends. I am sure once I talk to Ammi's family and explained your financial situation, there will not be a problem."

Ziljan sat back in his chair and smiled. "Now to your invitation to join the priesthood singers, you already know it is an honor to be asked. Of course, you might already know our family has the Kohathite background."

"There's good and bad from our ancestors, but the good – and best – part of our heritage is the singing. Kings David and Solomon, as well as King Jehosophat, loved music and it is through them that we were allowed to sing in the Temple and synagogues. David was the one who laid everything out for his son when he planned for the songs of praise in the Temple, for the ascent and the descent."

"As to you becoming a singer in the synagogue, I agree with the priests' request. Our family is a part of the Kohathite Levites. Music is in our blood. I, myself, play the flute and am proficient on the cymbals. When it is my orders' turn for music, I report to the synagogue in my area and render music."

"Priests are allowed to marry so I am quite sure your Ammi will be pleased for you. However, as far as you singing in the synagogue, I cannot help in your decision. That is something you must make for yourself."

14

The cousins talked until well into the evening. They found they had many things in common. Ziljan brought to Bartimaeus' memory a time when he and his father came to visit Bartimaeus' family.

"I believe this may have been the time your father asked mine to set up a trust for you. You had recently lost your sight and your mother had taken you from the room. Your father loved you so much. I remember he rose from his seat to hug you before you left the room. This may have been when you were about ten or eleven years of age — not sure which."

Bartimaeus vaguely remembered this occasion. "I could not see, but I seem to remember that I noticed your father's voice resembled my father's and that your voice was deeper than I thought it should be. How old were you, Ziljan?" he asked.

"I must have been a teenager, possibly 16 or 17. And you're right; my voice started changing at an early age." Ziljan rubbed his throat as he smiled.

"In fact, I think that is what some of the young ladies liked about me. My mother told me some thought it was a 'romantic voice,' but at that time I didn't know what she meant. I had been singing around my village as well as in the synagogue. Perhaps it is your voice which made Ammi take notice of you, Bartimaeus!" Both men laughed heartily at the remark.

"I had been singing hymns for a few years with my father around the house and at family gatherings before my blindness, and I already knew Ammi for our families were friends." Bartimaeus smiled in return.

"Of course, some of the people think I'm too loud, or I sing the same song for too long a time. Yet, if I really enjoy certain songs, I tend to sing them over and over. There are, of course, those who enjoy my singing if it's also their favorite song. When I know the song is being enjoyed, I continue to sing and my alms are increased. My singing also brings more coins for my friends, so I also sing for them."

Ziljan looked directly into his cousin's face. "You know, of course, that your income from the alms is now cut off. You don't have to do that any more. You've always been quite wealthy, you know."

"Oh, yes! I've always known that because of the trust, but the money I received went to help my friends who needed the money more than myself. There are those who do not receive enough alms to eat or have a place to stay, so I make sure that I can spread the wealth."

"Yes, I've come to see how helpful you've been to others. The Lord will reward you, I know. I also see you've allowed some of your friends to live in your small house near the synagogue."

Bartimaeus nodded his head. "When the rains appear there are a few beggars who have no home or shelter so I've always made room for them. That is one of the stipulations I gave to my friends, Jonas and Nathan, when I invited them to live in the house — that they allow those who sat with us near the synagogue an opportunity to stay dry. Of course, there are those who have families and places for shelter, so there is never more than two or three who accept such hospitality."

The two men enjoyed each other's company and eventually knew if they were to get started early in the morning, it was best to continue getting to know each other at another time.

Ziljan offered Bartimaeus the opportunity to stay over for the night, but Bartimaeus knew he had a lot to think over. He wanted to sit in his own home to do serious thinking. By the time Bartimaeus took his leave, the sun had begun to set and he felt as if a weight had been taken off his shoulders.

The next day they planned to meet with the servants who used to report to his father at his family's home.

He and his cousin would soon approach Ammi's father within a fortnight to discuss betrothal arrangements. Now his only worry was whether or not his proposal would be accepted by her family.

15

For four days, Bartimaeus and Ziljan traveled throughout his property. There were shepherds, groomsmen, and gardeners to be retained. He met many of his late parents' servants and was pleased he could still remember many of them. At one point, he sat with some of the servants he remembered from his youth, and learned of the passing of a few of the previous elderly servants. They also related children who had been born since his blindness, the work that had been added to his home or torn down, and other news, bringing him up-to-date since he had gone to live in town. All mentioned they had been adequately paid by his man of business.

When Ziljan prepared to introduce his cousin's house servants, Bartimaeus smiled, and acknowledged many of them by name.

"We are so happy to know that you can see again and have always prayed for your healing. Many of us have seen Jesus the Healer and have listened to his teachings. When Ziljan told us of your healing and that you would be returning to your family home, we were so very pleased! Welcome home, young lord!"

Bartimaeus realized there was some hesitation by his mother's now elderly housekeeper, Retha, and her family.

There was a question on her face that was not spoken and it was not long before he realized she and other members of her family wished to remain as his servants.

He put his arms around Retha's thin shoulders. This was the woman who used to feed him sweets and rocked him to sleep. When his mother was ill, she was her nurse. Without being asked, he expressed to the group he would be happy if they would consider staying on and continue with their previous duties. He could see this pleased all of them.

Ziljan seemed pleased with the way Bartimaeus was handling the business concerning the retaining of his servants.

"First thing," he said with a smile, "it would be wonderful to once again have some decent meals coming from the kitchen." The group laughed as Retha said, "Young man, you will eat like a king this evening!"

He reached into a leather bag at his waist and gave her a small pouch. "I know you'll need funds to purchase meat and vegetables for the house. I'm sure there's enough money for the entire household for tonight and the rest of the week. I'll also make sure you have enough to purchase dishware and eating utensils for I'm told there are no kitchen items."

Retha's husband, Simeon, looked at his wife and then turned a smiling face toward Bartimaeus. "Sir, do not worry about such items. We removed them when your parents died so that no one would come into the house to steal. They are packed at our house, as well as some of your mother's special materials and curtains. We will begin righting your house starting in the morning. Nothing needs to be purchased right now. We also have items from your old room as well."

Simeon looked very sad as he said, "We are so sorry for the loss of your parents and the small ones. The sickness that went through the village killed many people that year. Your mother was very weak following the babies' births and your father mourned your mother's death. There were two boys born, both within one year. But we are very happy you, as the heir, have returned."

16

Arrangements had been made by Bartimaeus to rent a small wagon with a mule so that neither would have to walk home in the dark after their meeting with Ammi's father. He planned to pick up Ziljan and they would travel together to discuss and make arrangements for the betrothal meeting.

Bartimaeus and Ziljan traveled to the outskirts of town after the sun had been in the sky for a few hours. The heat of the day had not occurred as yet and they talked as the mule slowly pulled the wagon.

"This is a beautiful area, Bartimaeus." Ziljan looked around at the herds of sheep and cattle and the lush farmland."

"Yes, Ammi's father is quite well-to-do. This is his property and those are his animals. On the other side of this you'll find more cattle, horses and mules on rich pastureland. It is one of the reasons her father and brothers want Ammi to not only marry well, but to also be well taken care of. There are men who desire her hand in marriage because of her family's wealth. Her betrothed who died was a bit older than Ammi and seemed to like her, but he was wealthy also. I really believe he was trying to marry in order to have heirs as well as obtain more land."

"I know her father was thinking of his daughter's security as well that she not be taken advantage of. Of course, Ammi's brothers would make sure no harm would come to her." He chuckled and soon began to laugh very hard.

"What's so funny?" Ziljan asked.

"When I was blind and Ammi would visit me beside the synagogue, there would always be one of her brothers somewhere nearby. She was always well protected – even against a blind man. I don't think she even realized one was nearby, but I could sense, smell and hear them. My eyesight may have been gone, but my other senses are very acute. On her way to see me, her many suitors would stop to talk with her, or try to be her escort to the services."

"The oldest brother would be hiding behind buildings or a moving trader's cart. She has twin younger brothers; I couldn't see but I could certainly detect their footsteps for they have a distinctive type of sandal that no one else wears. Also, they wear distinct oils that no one else wears."

He continued to smile. "The family of Marcus Bentar has servants of trade whose jobs it is to make the family's special sandals, body and hair oils, clothes and whatever the family needs. They have trade servants who make their pottery with their names on the sides, as well as other servants who concoct the special oils. There are servants for just about everything — special pottery, robes, candles, wagons, fences — everything!"

"Ammi has learned how to mix her own oils and perfumes to the way she wants to smell each day. Chion, her servant, chaperone and friend, taught her many domestic lessons. She's very good with fabrics and dyes and is a good seamstress. She made a type of covering for my bed to keep me warm during cold nights, but had to quietly give it to me so her family would not find out. I never knew how beautiful it was until I received my sight. When I moved to my home, I brought it with me."

Bartimaeus stopped smiling and looked a bit worried. "Are you sure I have enough to offer for Ammi, Ziljan? After all, I am a man who once sat outside the synagogue singing and begging with the infirmed."

He wrinkled his nose in thought. "Ziljan, what about the dowry or the bride price? Am I to pay for Ammi? I've heard about them but never thought I would need to ask their meanings. What exactly are they? I don't know if I give them to her or she gives them to me."

With a smile on his face, Ziljan answered, "She gives it to you – either property or money. Don't fret yourself for you probably have as much, if not more, than Marcus Bentar. Do not worry, my cousin, do not worry! I will speak for you as your family representative. There really is nothing for you to do but look interested and if you agree with the discussion, just nod your head. Her father will handle the question and answer of dowry before the contract is signed."

"I'll be sitting beside you and should you feel the need to ask or explain anything, hold your hand out or just touch my knee and then speak. Stop worrying, Bartimaeus."

Ziljan gave a secretive smile as they continued on.

17

The wagon approached the house, which was spread over a great area and a manservant met them at the door. After they disembarked, a young groomsman took the wagon to the rear of the house. They could see bushes, flowers and fruit trees at the rear, and a small herd of horses were to the far right.

"Good morning, my lord Bartimaeus," the servant greeted them as he bowed toward them.

"I saw you coming from a long way off and decided to stay here to greet you."

Without turning his head, Ziljan threw a quick look at his cousin, who showed a bit of surprise at the greeting. Bartimaeus introduced his cousin and the two were invited inside. Clapping his hands, a young servant appeared and had them sit on stools beside the door. He immediately removed their sandals and calmly began to wash both of the men's feet. After drying, the young man disappeared and the manservant had them follow him down the long hall.

The two were then led to Ammi's father who was sitting at a table in a small greeting room. The room had warm tapestry and they could see a woman's touch throughout.

Since Ammi's mother passed away some time ago, Bartimaeus knew without asking that the feminine decorations and pottery on the shelves and interior had to be Ammi's work. She once discussed with him some of the decorations she had added to her father's study and knew she loved weaving tapestry. Pillows were interspersed throughout with brass candlesticks and bowls of incense on the table. At each area of the room there were fruit bowls. Even though the windows allowed sunlight to come in, a few of the candles were lit, presumably offering a soft reading light.

As they entered the room, Bartimaeus caught a glimpse of Ammi on the other side of a stuccoed wall. He smiled at her and she shyly returned the smile before backing up a few feet behind the wall.

A slender dark-skinned woman of possibly Ethiopian heritage appeared beside her, who touched Ammi's shoulder. The two turned and slowly sauntered toward the rear of the house. Bartimaeus realized the woman must be Chion, whom Ammi had mentioned many times. Chion seemed to watch out for her charge with love and was possibly more than a housekeeper, servant or nurse.

Ammi whispered something to the woman who calmly turned to look at him and his cousin and then back to Ammi. He noticed she had beautiful dark eyes with long lashes. Her look was not piercing, but contemplative. She nodded to Ammi as if agreeing with something that was said. Both smiled at one another, continuing their walk down the hall.

The women gave one last look at the roomful of men, then turned toward an open hallway and disappeared from his view.

18

Bartimaeus turned toward Ammi's father as he and Ziljan continued toward him. Ammi's father, who missed nothing, saw the exchange between his daughter, Bartimaeus, and then her handmaiden and gave a slight smile as he pushed back from the table.

A little older and a little grayer, he looked pretty much the same as Bartimaeus remembered him from his youth. He still had the stance of a man with presence. Bartimaeus knew he would recognize Ammi's father anywhere. He noticed Marcus' muscular build and realized he was still a fit man. He wondered if his father would have still looked the same had he lived to reach this age.

"Ah, Bartimaeus bar Timaeus. It is good to see you and to know that you can see me also." There was humor in his statement.

Although he knew Ammi and Bartimaeus had been friends since childhood, Marcus Bentar had tried to stem the relationship because he wanted his daughter to be happy. He knew the Timaeus family was quite well-to-do, yet he did not want to see his daughter leading a blind man to the synagogue each day to beg. He had voiced this to her, but Ammi had adamantly told him she would not mind doing so. Servants and valets could be hired for that purpose, but he knew Ammi would be the one to lead him around.

He thought the first betrothal would settle the quandary. Unfortunately, the young man died of a childhood disorder and he watched how Ammi mourned him. There was no actual sadness in her eyes, but out of respect for his family and according to custom she wore mourning clothes for the full year.

Ammi's brothers were not overly concerned about the relationship of the blind man and their sister, although Marcus generally sent one or all three to check on her whenever she went to town.

Many times Ammi would request Chion to go along rather than her brothers. Her brothers were not afraid that Bartimaeus would take advantage of their sister, but only wanted to make sure she was happy. She was always circumspect and most times wore the veil, but knew she removed it when she approached him. They weren't really worried because, after all, the man was not able to see. They noticed she always seemed happiest when she returned from visiting with Bartimaeus.

Chion enjoyed traveling outside of the house with Ammi, for it gave her time to visit with friends and other servants. She could watch Ammi from a distance in the event she felt Ammi wanted personal time with Bartimaeus and would calmly wait for her to rejoin her for the return home.

Ammi appreciated Chion's calm spirit for she never took advantage of her authority. Bartimaeus could not see or hear her, but knew Chion was never far away from her charge and appreciated the fact that she allowed a modicum of privacy for the two young people.

Unbeknownst to Bartimaeus and Marcus Bentar, Chion understood the situation and did not worry about him taking advantage of her charge.

19

Ah, thought Bartimaeus, this looks to be a most pleasant meeting. Some of his nervousness began to slowly disappear.

Yesterday Ziljan had dispatched a servant with a message about the time of their arrival and presumably the subject of what would be discussed at the meeting. He was sure his cousin had mentioned the subject of a marriage proposal. Bartimaeus still wondered if Ziljan had mentioned anything about the bride price since he was unaware of the ramifications of asking for a woman's hand in betrothal or marriage.

Marcus Bentar stood to greet the two men and introductions were made. When he looked at Ziljan, a flash of remembrance showed in his eyes.

"You must be Shiloh, my friend Ziljan's son, and I can see the family resemblance. I remember you from your bar mitzvah years ago, and later at your wedding, which was a joyous affair. It's been a long time. Sit, sit," he said as he gestured them toward two chairs, one on each side of the table.

The preliminaries over, they launched into the betrothal discussion which quickly took place and Ziljan did most of the talking. All Bartimaeus had to do was nod his head in agreement and smile. There were times he felt somewhat silly, but tried to look serious as he remembered Ziljan's instructions.

Within the hour, the men went outside to the village gates not far from the house. The older men who sat beside the gate looked up and smiled at the three men. Within minutes a sandal was transferred from Ziljan's hand to Bartimaeus' hand and later to Marcus' hand, signifying a proposal had been made and accepted.

The men headed back to Marcus's house and all were smiling. Bartimaeus was now the betrothed of Ammi and there would be a celebration of *eyrusin*. Their wedding would take place in the very near future.

20

Upon entering the main room, Marcus clapped his hands twice and Ammi's nurse came to the door.

"Chion, please bring Ammi to me," he directed with a smile. Chion smiled in return and hurried to do his bidding.

A few moments later Chion escorted her charge as Ammi shyly entered the room and returned the smiles of the three men, her brothers and her nurse.

Chion could feel Ammi trembling beside her and felt her charge's hand slip into hers. She gave a quick squeeze to Ammi's hand and it was quickly returned.

Not long after the women's arrival, her father relayed to Ammi that Bartimaeus had requested her hand in marriage and he had given his consent. The request had been agreed upon, the bride price had been set, agreed upon, and sealed this day.

Ziljan explained that Bartimaeus has been made aware of the requirements of the betrothal and the time of separation of the couple prior to the wedding, to which Marcus nodded his head in pleased agreement.

Bartimaeus informed the group that he had started the process of hiring servants for his home and preparing new living quarters by adding onto his property. It was his plan to leave the final furnishings to Ammi when they were wed.

A few minutes later, Ammi's three brothers entered the room and introductions were made by Marcus. Ziljan believed all three had been made aware of the betrothal and was of the opinion they agreed wholeheartedly. Bartimaeus did not say anything, but knowing Ammi's siblings, believed they may have listened from somewhere nearby.

"Father," the eldest asked, "does this mean we can stop following our sister around whenever she chooses to go away from the house?"

The men gave a great laugh at this remark to which Marcus gave an exaggerated wink. Both Bartimaeus and Ammi looked a bit embarrassed but joined in.

A rustling noise and conversations were then heard outside the meeting room. A priest was then ushered in by the same manservant who greeted Bartimaeus and Ziljan at the door. The priest stood aside and held his hand out toward the door as two more priests entered.

Bartimaeus was happy to see that one of the priests was his good friend, Eliud, and the two men smiled at one another.

The contract was then signed and exchanged in their presence and an announcement of the betrothal was made. Following the blessings by the priests, wine was then passed around. When Ammi received hers, she turned and gave it to her servant.

"Father, Bartimaeus," she started and then hesitated. "When I am wed, may I bring my Chion with me to my new home?" She looked at Chion, who had taken the cup and smiled. Bartimaeus could only guess that a discussion had previously taken place between Chion and Ammi. There was more than friendship between the two and he could see their love for each other. Although perhaps only a decade separated the two women, he could see that Chion was like a second mother to Ammi.

Both Marcus and Bartimaeus nodded their heads in the affirmative. Bartimaeus knew his wife would need a loyal woman by her side after they were wed – and who better than Chion? He thought of his late mother and her friend and confidant, Retha.

Ammi had once explained that Chion had been hired when her mother was alive. Chion had a husband, who died during a raid on her village and she was captured. She said she was pregnant during the raid, but lost the baby. She was sold as a slave by her captors, but her father purchased and released her from slavery. She requested to remain with him and immediately became his most loyal servant. She gave loving care to his late wife during her illness, ran his household, and was a great comfort to him and his children following her passing.

When she came to Marcus Bentar's household, she nursed his wife until her death as well as helped to raise Ammi during her childhood.

Following her mother's death, it was Chion who was her comfort during that time. Ammi loved her and did not want to have to look for a new handmaiden.

Chion and Ammi had talked long into the night the evening after Bartimaeus received his sight. Ammi knew he was only a few years older than she, and that he had feelings for her, but because of his new social status would have to consider taking a wife and having a family.

Her older brother, Matthew, had once explained to her that he remembered from his youth that Bartimaeus' family had not been poor, but he was unaware of the blind man's financial status. He remembered the man's parents had died, but was also aware they had been very well off and owned a lot of property. If there was any inheritance, Bartimaeus would be the sole heir.

"Someone must have purchased a small house for Bartimaeus because he did not sleep on the streets," he had informed her.

"Although many beggars live on the streets and in doorways, Bartimaeus always had someplace to go in the evenings. I once sneaked inside and saw that the small house was nicely furnished, although chairs and tables had spaces between them." He believed this was because the blind man had to have space to maneuver since he could not see.

Ammi told Chion that she had been praying that since he now had sight, Bartimaeus would be able to ask for her in the near future. It was at this point that she asked Chion to come with her should he do so. When it looked like her prayers were being answered, Chion had told her she would love to stay with her if her father and her betrothed agreed.

"After all, I am the servant of your father and besides," the older woman had jokingly responded, "if you married and I remained here, I'd be stuck with your three teasing brothers, and what need would they have for me?"

Her eldest brother, Matthew, was already betrothed and in a few years would be leaving the household. The twins had previously celebrated their bar mitzvahs and were already courting many of the area's girls in their age group. They would make great matches, for the Bentars were well known in the area.

"Is that all right with you, Chion?" Marcus asked. He was aware that Chion loved Ammi and would follow his daughter any where.

She lifted her eyes to Marcus, who nodded his head, gave a great laugh and said, "If Chion wishes to go with you, then I have no problem. Of course I'll have to start looking for a new housekeeper to make sure my home continues to run smoothly. She has been nurse, housekeeper and confidant, as well as a good friend to my wife before she died. I guess we'll have to make sure we find someone soon so Chion can train her during your betrothal period." He smiled at both women.

Chion returned his smile and smiled at the other men; once again she lowered her eyes as she sipped the wine, but she knew in her heart it was what she wanted. She loved Ammi very much and knew Bartimaeus would make her very happy.

She began silently and mentally planning the next step toward Ammi's wedding. Chion decided right then she would use her extra time to help with Ammi's trousseau, for a year goes by very quickly when it comes to a wedding. She and Ammi's friends would work hard to make sure Ammi did not want for anything during the period of her betrothal. Ammi could possibly have four or five maids in her procession, but since she was popular in the community, Chion was also aware that there could possibly be ten to twelve.

21

Chion was not entirely surprised that Bartimaeus wanted to marry Ammi, yet as she thought back to few years ago, what really surprised her was before Bartimaeus was healed, Ammi had tearfully confided to her that if it was possible, she would much rather be betrothed to Blind Bartimaeus than to Samuel. When her father made the pronouncement of her betrothal to Samuel, she remembered her charge was very sad for the days following.

Truthfully, Ammi had admitted she did not dislike Samuel, but she was not really interested in him. They had very little in common for he was almost eight years older and she found him to be somewhat cold and commanding. After visiting his household and meeting his parents, she began to realize that her married life would be a lonely one — for she would no longer have the freedoms she enjoyed and saw her life as a woman in prison. Samuel's mother was a quiet woman of courtesy who welcomed her into the family, but even she was hardly seen in public.

Samuel had voiced his opinion concerning her visits to the blind man long before the betrothal took place and later, when they drank the betrothal wine, he began quietly reciting to her the do's and don'ts of what was expected of his wife.

Along with her family, Samuel had once walked beside her to the synagogue for a special Sabbath service and when she stopped to say hello to Bartimaeus, he had territorially grabbed her arm to keep her moving in a direction away from the line of beggars. Her father and brothers acknowledged Bartimaeus and her father had dropped coins into the cups and bowls of his and a few other beggars near him.

Bartimaeus knew Ammi's steps and without seeing, immediately knew her newly-betrothed had moved her way from the beggars' area.

Her twin brothers, Simon and Joseph, did not miss watching their sister's action of quietly withdrawing from his touch. Wise beyond their years at that time, they were very observant. They would soon celebrate their bar mitzvahs, but felt they were already men because their father entrusted them with some of his business, knowing their capabilities.

Unbeknownst to the family, they had discussed the matter among themselves when they went to their shared bed quarters later that evening.

"Father should know that Samuel is not the right man for our sister," observed Simon.

"I know," Joseph answered. "I'm not sure if I like him myself. I find him too domineering! Did you notice how Ammi seems to always keep him at a distance? Even

Matthew should see she's not very happy about marrying that man."

Simon patted his cheek with his forefinger as he pondered the matter.

"I know. Don't forget, he'll soon be our brother-in-law. He's not like Abel, Riyadah's husband, who is friendly. They don't live close by and when they visit, it is as if he's been part of our family for years. Besides, Riyadah's due any day now and they plan to return to our home with the baby after the birth. If it's a boy, we'll see them even sooner for the child's *bris*.† Now that will be a grand celebration. We'll be uncles!" The brothers smiled at this statement.

Matthew had also seen his sister withdraw her arm. Samuel was his friend, but upon their betrothal, he was seeing the man in a different light.

Although her father accepted the betrothal request, even he knew Ammi's heart would never be given to Samuel. She was an obedient daughter and he knew she would be an obedient wife but she would not be a happy one.

Marcus thought of his own betrothal to his dead wife, Rebar. She was a beautiful woman, loving, full of light and laughter and highly intelligent. Rebar was the perfect hostess, and kept his household in smooth running order. She was wise in business and she had taught Ammi to use her business head in certain areas. When she walked into a room, a pleasant atmosphere came with her.

Ammi resembled his late wife so much in looks and temperament that there were times he thought Ammi would eventually resemble Rebar when she was older. She did not attend the Jewish schools as her brothers, but by sitting with Matthew while he studied, she had learned to read and could perform mental figuring faster than Matthew. Marcus was very proud of his daughter's intelligence.

His other daughter, Riyadah, was also very intelligent, but used her knowledge in keeping house and being dutiful to her husband. She was a loving and diligent wife to Abel and, like Ammi, was always very happy.

He really wanted Ammi to also be happy for she was the light of his life. He was sorry Samuel took ill and died, but he noticed her love for the blind man brought her joy; he began to believe this engagement to Bartimaeus may have been the Lord's will. His elder daughter had made a love match with her betrothal and marriage and he wanted the same for his younger daughter.

On this day, Ammi was radiant and even his sons seemed in favor and in agreement with today's betrothal. He always felt the twins accepted the first betrothal, but believed neither of them had been very fond of Samuel. Although Matthew was a friend of Samuel, even he did not seem to be as happy for his sister after that announcement was made.

22

The family celebrated late into the evening before Ziljan and Bartimaeus took their leave. Ziljan gave a sideways glance at his cousin and smiled. Bartimaeus had a lopsided smile on his face and a slightly noticeable skip to his walk.

"Happy now, my cousin?" Ziljan asked.

"My, yes! How things have changed over the space of a few months." They walked out the front of the house to wait for the groom to re-hitch the wagon to take them home.

Bartimaeus thought back to the loss of his sight, his healing by Jesus, meeting of his cousin, and now the betrothal to his beloved friend, Ammi.

He turned toward Ziljan and smiled. "Thank you so much for standing with me and explaining my financial situation. When you gave information of my financial business, I saw Marcus' eyebrows shoot to the top of his forehead. Even I was not aware of the exact amount and I think my eyebrows went up also." The two men began laughing at this remark.

It was growing dark and both agreed the meeting went well and planned to meet in a few months to begin wedding plans. The cousins reached the front courtyard on Marcus Bentar's property. They idly conversed as they began walking behind the servant to the livery stable to meet the groom with the wagon that would carry them to their respective homes.

23

The day dawned bright and clear and there was the sweet smell of incense in the hallways and under the arches of the synagogue. The priests had lined themselves near the openings and he could see Eliud, as well as Shemiah and the other priests standing along the sides.

The priests would be singing during the ceremony and, beginning the end of the next month, he would be among them – for he had given his answer and would be placed in the choir. Already Shemiah had given him a new song to learn where he would perform as one of the soloists.

Ammi had seven maids, which included her sister, Riyadah, and Azemi, Ziljan's wife, who flowed down the synagogue's aisle toward him. Bartimaeus' cousin and the men who had begged alms with him followed the procession. The men had bathed, trimmed their beards and wore clean robes. Bartimaeus hardly knew his two friends, for he had never seen them arrayed in such a manner.

Jonas and Nathan stood beside Ziljan and almost the entire village was present.

Ziljan had arrived two months prior to the wedding. Along with him came his wife, Azemi, other relatives of Bartimaeus, whom he had never met, and numerous servants. Bartimaeus felt good knowing he had more family and they all seemed to look very prosperous. When they arrived, Marcus Bentar was pleased to see men he had once known in his youth, who had since moved to other areas. He also had a lot of catching up to do with old friends who had moved from the valley. It was almost a family reunion for both sides.

Bartimaeus' house was full of relatives and it seemed a party was held every night. Two days prior to the wedding, a large house was rented for the family, for he would be bringing his bride to his house following the ceremony.

Ziljan's servants joined with his servants during the day and all began sprucing up his house and preparing food for the wedding celebration. Cousins brought new curtains and dishware to be placed on shelves. Ammi's bridesmaids also arrived and began placing feminine objects around the house. Most of the objects were items her maids knew she liked and those that Ammi had purchased herself for her new home.

As he made a quick glance around the large hall, he smiled at his newly-introduced relatives and friends. He looked at the bridesmaids and each gave him a wide smile. His heart was full to bursting.

His eyes went to the priestly singers and saw Eliud and Shimea laughing together. The priestly choir sang a special love song for the couple prior to the bridesmaids' courtly walk to the altar.

His new father-in-law was happy as he looked at his lovely daughter. Her gown was simple but elegant. Chion and Ammi had worked steadily, day and night, on the gown for at least two weeks. Chion refused to let the other servants work with the material, which was purchased through the Chinese traders, directly following the betrothal ceremony. The silks and linen materials were placed lovingly across chairs and tables in the preparation room.

One thing Marcus knew, he could always rely on Chion to handle the business of his daughter's wedding. Chion was a great haggler. She set a price between high and low, giving her leeway to bargain an amount that she felt was acceptable to the traders. Since they had bargained with her before, they knew what Chion would like for her charge's wedding. After transacting the purchases, both gave wide smiles for business well done.

Bartimaeus had given funds to Chion and told her to purchase whatever Ammi needed that would make her happy. Unbeknownst to him, her father had also given Chion a large sum for the same reason. Being frugal, Chion and Ammi had no need to spend a large amount of their money for she also had her own funds from an inheritance of her late mother's family.

When Ammi and her sister were younger, their mother had set funds aside so that whenever Riyadah and Ammi were to marry, they would not have to scrimp and save.

Riyadah had come to stay prior to the wedding. Azemi had arrived with her husband weeks earlier. Riyadah, Azemi, and Ammi quickly bonded, which left Chion to happily work undisturbed. She was able to finish last-minute duties prior to the day of the wedding.

Marcus could hear them laughing and talking throughout the nights before the wedding. Many times during the week, he would go near their rooms late at night and tell them to get some rest, for there was much to do prior to the ceremony. After he left their rooms, he could still hear them giggling as he retreated down the hallway.

The women stayed at Marcus' home and talked and laughed together throughout the three days and nights prior to the wedding. Of course, on the day of the wedding, all of the maids would go into the room that was set aside for them to dress and prepare for the service.

Marcus could not stop smiling – mainly because he could see his daughter was very, very happy. The gold and silver chain he had given Ammi as one of his wedding presents to her was just the right accessory for her dress. It lay on her chest and matched the bangles on her arms, which reflected the gold thread throughout the material of her wedding dress. Riyadah and Azemi had arranged her hair and intertwined thin gold thread throughout her long braid and wrapped it in such a way as to place her veil. She positively shined when he first saw her this morning.

When Ziljan came to escort his wife to their rented house three days prior to the wedding, she looked so forlorn that Marcus and Bartimaeus requested that she be allowed to stay. While Riyadah, Azemi and her maids dressed and gave marriage advice to Ammi, Marcus praised Yahweh for his daughter's friends and new family.

* * *

Marcus was happy to hold his new grandson, and prayed that soon he would have more grandchildren from both his daughters and later, his son's wives when they married. Since Riyadah no longer lived close by, he was happy for his family to once again be together in the house. He enjoyed his many conversations with Abel, Riyadah's husband. Abel was a good man who loved his wife and new son; and Marcus was happy to see how he treated his eldest daughter. He admitted to himself that he was a very happy father today.

Female relatives and Ammi's friends had brought beautiful scarves, curtains, pottery, newly-made leather sandals to Ammi a month before the ceremony. She had laughed when she told the women that she did not have to spend any of her father's or Bartimaeus' money because she now had everything she needed to start her marriage.

The wedding dinner was sumptuous and included everything from various meats, fruits, vegetables and all types of breads and sweets, to the finest wines from Bartimaeus and Marcus Bentar's grape houses. Ziljan brought wines from his area and all made sure that the wine would not run out, for they knew the wedding celebration would last for many days.

Although Bartimaeus had broken the wedding cup during the ceremony, Ammi's twin brothers placed another wrapped cup on the floor at the celebration so that Bartimaeus could do it again. There was a lot of clapping and whistling by the guests when Bartimaeus again performed the tradition. Right away, the group of musicians happily broke into music for the celebration dance, knowing the wedding participants and guests would continue through the night.

EPILOGUE

Another year has passed as Bartimaeus and Ammi stood at the back of their now furnished home and overlooked the grassy area beyond. He had his arm across her shoulder and she had her arm around his waist.

"Just think, Bartimaeus," Ammi mused, "if it had not been for Jesus the Healer, this would never have been possible."

"I know," he answered, "Jesus is the reason that our lives have been changed in many ways. My life, my spirit, my sight and my future with you." He gave a satisfied sigh as he hugged her.

They stood together in companionable silence for some time. Then in a subdued tone, Bartimaeus began disclosing what he had heard this afternoon.

"I was in the synagogue listening to some of the scribes, and overheard that the religious leaders in Jerusalem have been plotting the death of Jesus. I am praying that the Lord will be with Him so that he may continue spreading the good news. I do not see where He has committed any crimes for He preaches and teaches love, harmony and oneness with the Father."

"Jesus has returned to some areas and perhaps He will pass this way again. We shall invite him to share a meal with us and we can show Him our new baby. It is because of him that our family is expanding." Ammi laughed and patted her expanding belly as Bartimaeus joined in.

In a few days, there would be a gathering at their home with other believers, including some of the priests and his friends, Nathan and Jonas. Since Jesus had passed through Jericho, He had gained many disciples. They met for fellowship and discussed the words of Jesus and what He had taught them. Nathan had met others who had been healed by Him and they and their families would join with them to testify and celebrate their own healings.

Lifting his voice, Bartimaeus turned his face toward Jerusalem and began to quietly sing a hymn of praise. Unable to contain his happiness, his tenor voice rose in crescendo across the valley.

Chion smiled to herself as she silently folded new material and began to wrap skeins of wool in preparation for making infant clothing for the new baby. She would soon have a small blessing to care for in a few months' time.

Lonnie-Sharon Williams is a graduate of Cleveland State University and a retired middle school teacher. Previously she was a paralegal-secretary at major corporations and law firms in Cleveland. She has been the recipient of many grants and awards in the teaching and legal fields. Ms. Williams is a biblical history buff and has been writing short stories, skits and poems since the age of 10. Her first published work, *"The Healings, Three Stories…"* has received national acclaim and was featured in 2013 at The International Christian Retail Show in Chicago, Illinois, the national Christian book display for booksellers and readers.

Ms. Williams loves to attend concerts and plays and listens to all forms of music. She performs as a character actor and liturgical dancer in churches and programs throughout the state. She has one adult son, Robert, and daughter-in-law, Clare, who are her greatest supporters. She and her cat, Mykal Jaksen, reside in Cleveland, Ohio.